THE
COLONY

The
Colony

by Thomas Carroll

SUNSTONE
PRESS

SANTA FE

Sunstone books may be purchased for educational, business, or sales promotional use. For information please write: Special Markets Department, Sunstone Press, P.O. Box 2321, Santa Fe, New Mexico 87504-2321.

Library of Congress Cataloging-in-Publication Data

Carrol, Thomas, 1957–
    The colony / by Thomas Carroll.—1st ed.
        p. cm
    ISBN 978-0-86534-295-4 (hardcover : alk. paper)
    ISBN 978-0-86534-379-5 (softcover : alk. paper)
        1. Boys—Fiction. I. Title.
    PS3553 .A76548 C65 1999
    813' .54—dc21

                                99-048827

WWW.SUNSTONEPRESS.COM
SUNSTONE PRESS / POST OFFICE BOX 2321 / SANTA FE, NM 87504-2321 /USA
(505) 988-4418 / ORDERS ONLY (800) 243-5644 / FAX (505) 988-1025

This book is dedicated to Sheri and the girls—
Shoshanna, Elena, and Olivia

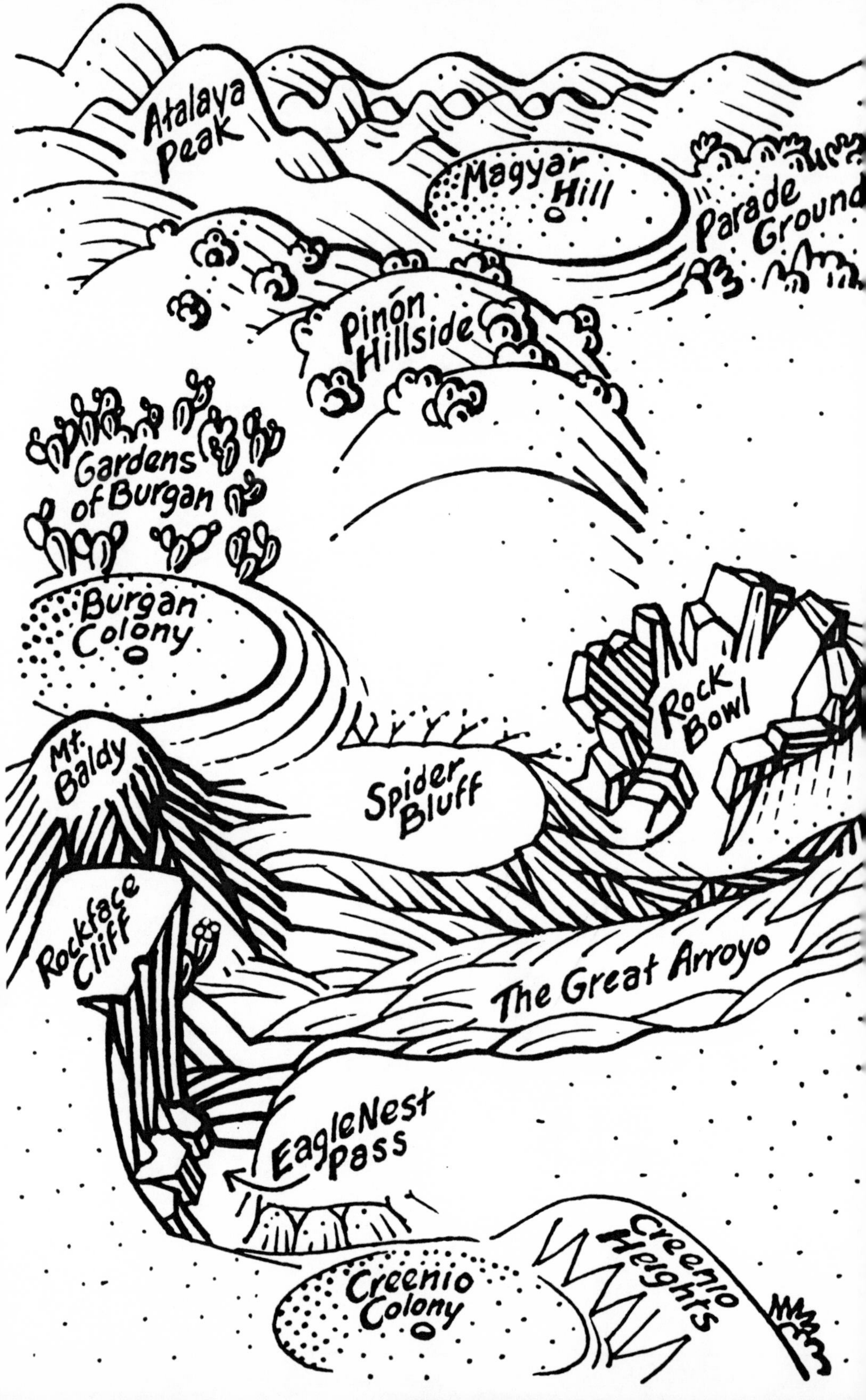

Atalaya Peak
Magyar Hill
Parade Ground
Pinon Hillside
Gardens of Burgan
Burgan Colony
Rock Bowl
Mt. Baldy
Spider Bluff
Rockface Cliff
The Great Arroyo
EagleNest Pass
Creenio Heights
Creenio Colony

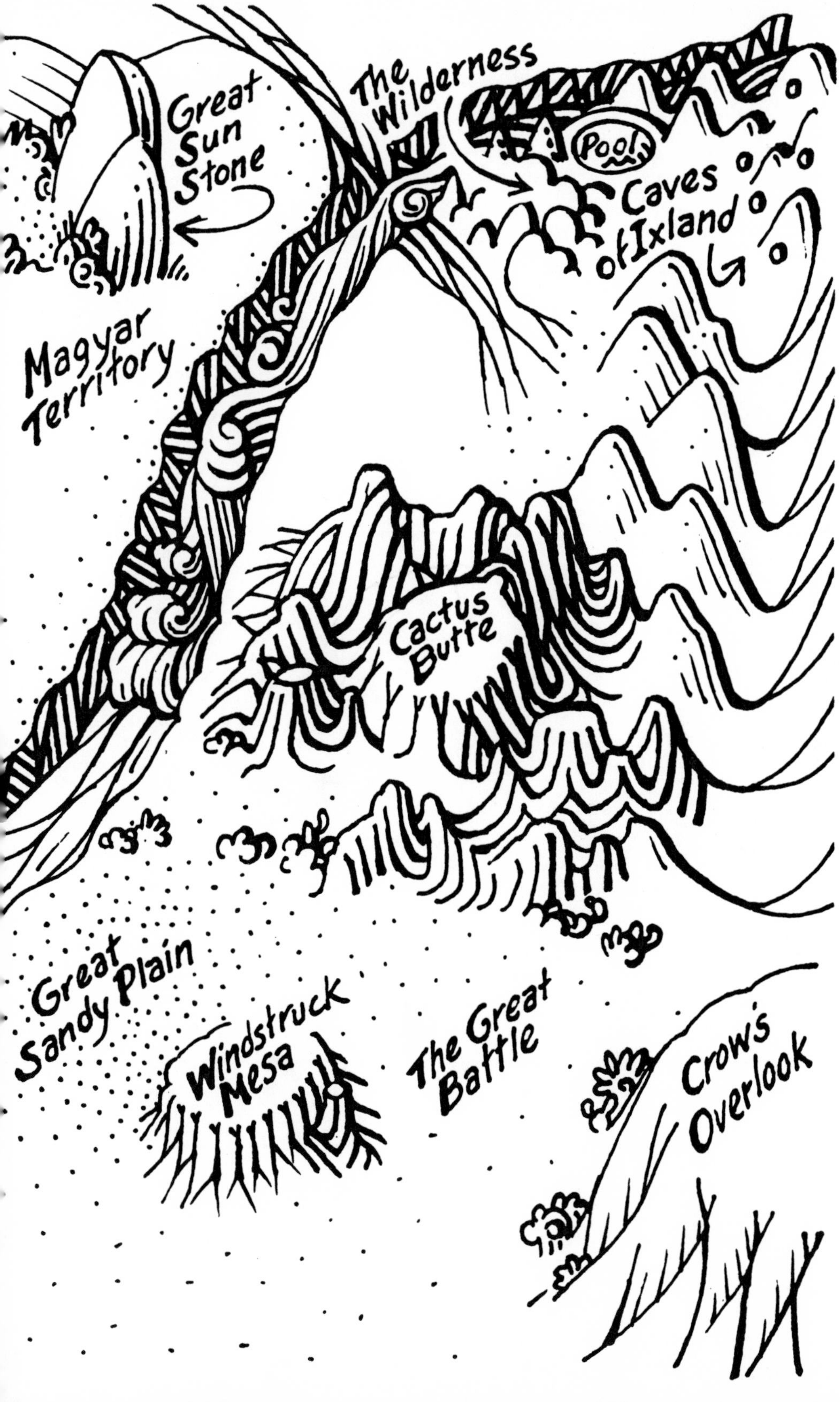
Great Sun Stone
The Wilderness
Pools
Caves of Ixland
Magyar Territory
Cactus Butte
Great Sandy Plain
Windstruck Mesa
The Great Battle
Crow's Overlook

1

"Lawrence, get off that computer right now. You're late. Lawrence! Answer me!"

His mother was calling from upstairs. He didn't answer. She probably has the car keys in her hand, waiting for me at the top of the stairs, he thought. But he was four levels down now, in the heart of the ant kingdom, and he had just fended off an attack by ten red ants. Two more levels down and he'd capture the queen.

"You'll be late for school!" she yelled.

"Just a minute, Mom," he called.

"NOT just a minute," she boomed back.

Her voice faded out. The screen darkened and suddenly three fire ants came at him. Click, click, click on the mouse— and he was safe and they were dead, torn apart. He immediately raced down a tunnel and found himself in a chamber filled with seeds. Wrong way! Go back! But the red ants blocked the tunnel. Trouble. His mother appeared at the doorway.

"I'll be late for my aerobics class," she snapped. In her hand she held a half-eaten protein bar with the wrapper pulled back.

"I already told you, I'm not going to school," said Lawrence.

"Lawrence, we've been through this," she sighed.

"I'm not going."

"He's not going to bother you today," she said.

"He bothers me everyday, Mom. All right, level five!"

"I talked to the principal."

"It didn't help." He went down a tunnel and into a huge chamber filled with ants.

"I'll talk to him again . . . after aerobics."

One tiny ant jumped out of a tunnel and yelled, "Follow me." Friend or foe? Lawrence had to decide. Go, he decided. The little ant turned out to be a friend and took him into the main chamber. Water was gushing in.

"Oh, no—a flood!"

His mother abruptly reached over and turned off the computer.

"Mom, I didn't even get to save it," he moaned. "Why'd you do that?"

"Because it's time to go."

"I could have saved it and played later," Lawrence said.

"Well, it's too late now. Let's go." She marched from the room.

His lunch was waiting on the counter upstairs.

"You've got a ride to soccer today, right?" said his mom. "So I'll pick you up there."

"If I'm still alive," he said. He threw the balled-up lunch into his backpack.

"Lawrence," said his mother softly. "You have to learn not to be afraid of him."

"He's going to kill me, Mom. He will, I know he will. He's got a gang."

"There aren't gangs in fifth grade. Not yet anyway."

"Well then, what are they?" replied Lawrence. "They follow him around and they'll kill me if he tells them to. That's a gang."

"If they give you a problem, just tell Mr. Ortega."

"I've told him a thousand times. He doesn't do anything."

"Tony's just a bully," said his mother. "Ignore him. He's not going to hurt you. Now you hurry along, or you'll be late," she said softly. "First give me a kiss."

Lawrence collected his backpack and left. It was almost eight o'clock. School started at eight-fifteen, but if he went the regular way he knew Tony would be waiting, so he headed out across the desert. The sun was coming over the mountains. The long arms of the cholla cactus reached towards the sun, their needles razor-sharp. It was late spring so the cactus flowers were in bloom. The desert was all purple and white. Cicadas were starting their morning song and it sounded like chain saws in the distance. The short, squat Spanish pines, or piñon trees, were perfectly still except for the flickers darting from branch to branch.

The dirt road had waist-high weeds growing up the sides, giant tangles of tumbleweeds and yellow-flowered shoots. Great foothills filled with piñon trees rose up before the Sangre de Cristo Mountains and the ski mountain. The leaves were just out, light green and glittering, so the whole mountainside surged gently back and forth.

At the top of the hill, things opened up. From the rise he could see Los Alamos in the distance and the Indian pueblo in the valley and the road leading to the Rio Grande. The plain before the river was filled with cacti and chamisa and sage, great clumps of it everywhere. The arroyo, filled with fine bleached sand, meandered its way to the river. It was dry now, but only until the rains came again, when it would fill with a fierce torrent of water, if only for a short time. In the heart of the valley, the Rio Grande wove its way through the trees and farms. The river itself was visible only in glimpses here and there. But Lawrence could see its path because of the tall trees that grew around it. In the high mountain desert the only tall trees grew around water, which was scarce. The piñons needed almost none. They were short, old trees, and they sat on the hillside like elderly men watching over the valley.

The desert stretched out endlessly. Lawrence had explored it many times, but always with his father. He was forbidden to go alone. "It's a wonderful, beautiful place, the desert," he said to his son, "but it's also dangerous. You couldn't survive out there on your own. It looks quiet, but it's filled with tarantulas, desert rats, rattlesnakes, cliffs that fall five hundred feet in one step, and cactus that'll rip your hand off. It's a place where you have to be a ready, or you will die."

"I'm ready," said Lawrence.

"One day you will be ready," his father had said. "Until then, never go into the desert alone."

Lawrence stopped. Something was moving among the trees. It was a man fording the river in a shallow place, getting wet up to his knees. An Indian, thought Lawrence. I wonder what he's doing coming in from the desert. He could see his strong forehead, dark skin, and long black hair braided behind him. Indian all right. He carried two black cases, both large, one held under each arm. I wonder what he's got in those cases? he asked himself.

While he was thinking, something zipped past his head. He wheeled but saw nothing. An arm rose above the chamisa and hurled another rock. Lawrence took off running. Another rock, a larger one this time, kicked up dirt in front of him, forcing him to pull up. Instantly, three boys stepped out from behind the trees. Manny and Ronny and Frankie Johnson. Tony's boys. Tony wasn't with them, but Lawrence knew he was there somewhere.

"Hey, Larry boy, we've been looking all over for you," said a voice. Tony stepped from behind a boulder. "Now, Larry, you know the rules," he said, tossing a rock into the air and catching it. "You walk to school the usual way and we wait for you and then we give you a hard time and then we all go to school. That's your job, to go the regular way so we don't have to be running all over the desert looking for you, and today you messed up. Big mistake."

"Just leave me alone," said Lawrence.

"Oh, sure, we'll leave you alone, won't we, guys?" It was the signal they were waiting for. They all cranked back and let fly. Two rocks whizzed by his head. One hit him in the shoulder. The pain shot through his left side.

"Just leave me alone," Lawrence repeated, rubbing his shoulder.

"Just leave me alone, just leave me alone," Tony mocked. "I will not. And if you rat on us again to Mr. Ortega I'm going to have to use this on you." Tony pulled a large hunting knife from a leather sheath attached to his belt.

Lawrence tried to slow the beating in his chest. "You're not allowed to have that in school," said he in a high squeaky voice, his throat closing up.

"We're not in school now, Larry boy, are we?" said Tony, laughing. And they all laughed with him. Lawrence looked at his flaming red hair, never washed, and his freckled face, twisted with laughter, and the knife. "He'll use it on me," he said to himself. "He's not human. He's a monster, he'll kill me."

"Want a cigarette, Larry boy? Come on, have a cigarette!" said Tony.

"I don't smoke."

"I don't smoke." Tony mocked his wimpy voice.

Tony took out a pack of Marlboros and peeled off the plastic wrap. He took one out and lit up. It dangled from his lips and the smoke went up into his face and eyes. As he squinted and twisted his face from the smoke, he looked like some hideous insect.

"Come on, have a cig, Larry boy."

"N-n-no!"

"You only have to say it once, Larry boy," said Tony. The boys laughed. "Larry, do you think this is sharp?" he said, rubbing his thumb over the blade of the knife.

"I'm late for school." His chest was shaking.

"Come on, let's make Larry boy have a cig."

The boys got hold and held him down while Tony took his lit cigarette and jammed it into Lawrence's mouth. "Smoke it, smoke it," yelled Tony. "Do it."

"Leave me alone," whined Lawrence. "Get off me!"

"Just smoke it and we'll leave you alone," said Tony, cramming it into his lips.

The cigarette burned his lip. It hurt so much he ripped free of them in one fierce move. His face was streaming with tears that he couldn't hold back.

"Oh, no, little Larry is crying," said Frankie Johnson.

"Did we make you cry?" said Manny. "We're so sorry."

"Wait till we tell your girlfriend," said Ron.

"You shut up," screamed Lawrence.

"Oh, did we say something wrong?" said Tony. "Well, hey, she thinks you're an idiot anyway."

"Shut up. And she's not my girlfriend," said Lawrence, through the tears.

"Sophia only hangs around with you because she feels sorry for you," said Tony.

Lawrence was stunned. The knife didn't scare him anymore. His face grew hot.

"Look, he's blushing," said Ron. "Little Larry boy is blushing."

"What a twerp," said Tony. "This is pathetic. I'm out of here. Come on, he's making us late for school. You tell Mr. Ortega, and I'm gonna use this knife on you." He held the knife up to his face. "You got that?"

Lawrence just stared at the ground.

"We're going this way," said Tony, pointing to the road. "Don't follow us."

"And just how am I supposed to get to school?"

"I don't care," said Tony. "Go walk in the Rio Grande for all I care. But not this road. This is my road. So get out of here."

He swung the knife around and Lawrence turned and scrambled down into the arroyo, the boys laughing at him all the way.

"See you, Larry boy," shouted Tony. "Don't step on any rattlesnakes."

The halls were empty when he arrived at school. Moments later, the whole class turned as he entered his homeroom class. He slumped down without a word, not daring to look at the girl next to him. The bell rang for first period.

"I thought you were sick or something," said Sophia, coming over.

"I'm fine."

"Wanta walk with me to math?" she asked.

"No," he said.

"Why not?" she said, sensing something was wrong. "What's your problem?"

"Nothing." Lawrence put his head in his hands and slid down in his chair.

"Oh, I know what happened. Tony again, huh?" She smiled at him. "Come on, forget it. I'll walk you to first period."

"All right," he said, following her out, afraid to look into her face.

They walked in silence. He couldn't bring himself to speak to her but when she smiled at him Tony's words evaporated from his mind. Sophia could do that, with one little smile or a kind word. I don't care what Tony says, he thought. She's my friend and I'm not going to believe any of it.

Just then Tony stepped out from behind a locker.

"Hey, Sophia, whattaya hangin' out with this loser for?"

"Get lost, Tony," she said. "Haven't you made enough trouble for one day? Get out of here, or I'll go to the principal's office."

"Principal's a friend of mine," he replied.

"We're going to class."

"Hey, Sophia, a bunch of us are going to the mall tonight, maybe catch a movie or something," said Tony. "Want to come along?"

"No way."

"Why not?"

"Because I think you're disgusting, Tony."

"Really," said Tony, turning red. "Well, I think *he's* disgusting."

He reached out and grabbed Lawrence by the ear, twisting it, lifting him up so high his feet were almost off the floor.

"My ear! You're ripping it off," squealed Lawrence.

"If you don't like it, why don't you do something about it, you little wimp?" Tony responded. "Why don't you fight me? Because you're a wimp."

"Tony, let go of him," yelled Sophia.

"If you want me to let go, then say you'll go out with me to the movies," replied Tony.

"Tony, don't be a jerk."

"Fine, then how's this?" He lifted Lawrence even higher.

"I won't go!" she said.

"Is that the way it is?" asked Tony.

"Let go of him or I'm going to Mr. Ortega!" she commanded.

Abruptly Tony let go and Lawrence fell back against a locker and slid down, holding his ear.

"What do you hang around with this dweeb for anyway, Sophia?"

"Just get out of here, all right?" she said sharply.

"Oh, forget it," said Tony in disgust. "We're leaving." Ronny and Manny and Frankie followed him down the hallway, laughing loud enough for them to hear.

"Now we know why he's picking on you," she said. "Sorry."

But Lawrence couldn't face her, not after he had cried in front of her. He took off down the hall.

"Wait! Lawrence, wait!" she called after him. But he kept going, out of the school building, across the baseball field, and all the way home. He went right to his room and packed his things. He moved quickly because he worried that his mother might come home at any moment. He stuffed his backpack with a pair of jeans, a photo of his mother and father that he took out of its frame, his toothbrush, a book, a pocketknife, two t-shirts, a small silver soccer trophy that he got when his team won the championship, and a box of Band-Aids. From the kitchen he took a jar of peanut butter and bread, potato chips, some powdered doughnuts, and a bottle of water. He went back to his room, sat down and wrote this letter.

> *Dear Mom and Dad,*
>
> *I love you very much, so please try to understand. I can't go back to my school. Not with Tony there. I know you have to make me, but I just can't go again. So I'm leaving. I'll come back and see you when I'm 16 and don't have to go to school anymore.*
>
> *Love,*
> *Lawrence*
>
> *P.S. Don't worry, I'll be all right.*

He slipped out the back door, just in case his mom should drive up at that moment, and took off into the hills. They would be looking for him on the roads, he knew, so he headed up a dry arroyo and into the desert. He pulled his baseball cap down so the afternoon wind wouldn't catch it and carry it off into some rocky ravine.

He came to a cliff of green rock. There was no way around, so up he went and continued further into the desert. He passed through a field of giant cholla cactus, walking carefully to keep from getting speared by the long arms. He suddenly found himself in another arroyo, a great sandy wash, dry now but waiting to roar with rainwater in the next storm. The sand was soft. It was hard going. So he climbed out and onto a long flat rock leading to a ravine. Cliffs loomed on both sides.

Tch-tch-tch-tch-tch-tch-tch-tch-tch. Lawrence froze. The rattlesnake was coiled, about five yards away. It kept its head up, waiting for movement. His father's voice came to him. "Don't move or you'll get bit. Stay still or it'll strike." So he didn't move. The snake slithered towards him. But still he did not move. He closed his eyes as the rattler went past his foot, down the slope into the arroyo.

Now unfrozen, he kept on, into the desert. Stopping at the top of a cliff, with great boulders and heaps of cholla at the bottom, he leaned over and a warm gust of wind blew up the rock face, so strong he almost lost his cap. He sat down and drained more from his water bottle than he should have, he knew, but he was thirsty. He had been walking now several hours. He ate a peanut butter sandwich.

"I can't go back, I can't go back," he found himself repeating out loud, even before he realized that he was thinking about turning back. "They'll make me go back to school. I can't go back," he thought. "But where will I go? It'll be dark soon."

He thought of the Indian village at Pojoaque. He could get his dinner there and then camp down by the Rio Grande, just a few miles away. But he didn't know which way that was. He tried to get his bearings and then walked for a few more hours, seeing no towns. From the top of one hill, turning around, he could see the lights of Santa Fe. He stared at them for a long time and a deep sadness set in. He then turned slowly and headed deeper into the desert.

Where is the village? Where is it? I've got to find it. It's getting dark.

Night sounds filled the ravine where he was walking. The desert is much noisier in the night than in the day. Rats scrambled out of their holes, bats whooshed overhead, coyotes started their lonely night howling. Now things were heard but not seen. He stepped on something moving, a snake or spider, and jumped back and ran wildly in the opposite direction. He ran up and down the hills without any idea where he was going, just moving because he was afraid to stop in the darkness.

What have I done? What have I done? he thought. I'm a fool, an idiot! I've left my home and my friends and everyone—and done the one thing my father told me never to do—go alone into the desert. And at night! Am I crazy? What was I thinking? He drove the thought out of his mind. I had to go. I had to. Tony gave me no choice.

It was pitch black. No moon, not even a small one, showed the way. There was nothing now but deep darkness. He couldn't even see the outlines of the hillsides. He could still hear the animals and creatures scurrying around. He ran aimlessly, and tumbled and fell and rolled to the bottom of the ravine. He wasn't hurt badly but his arms were scraped and some loose skin was hanging from one hand.

Reaching for his Band-Aids, he realized that his backpack was gone. He couldn't find it in the dark. His hands and legs were shaking uncontrollably. What will I eat? How will I keep warm? The desert was cooling off. In no time it would be so cold he would freeze. I better get going, he thought. I've got to find somewhere to sleep.

Something ran in front of him. He couldn't see what it was in the dark, but he heard something. A rat? A tarantula? A coyote? It could be anything.

"I've got to get home," he said aloud. "They'll be worried about me."

He turned around and ran. That's it, I'll go home, he thought as he ran. I don't care anymore. I have to get home. Who cares about Tony? I just want to be home and in my room. But wait—how will I find my way? His hands burned from the fall. His mouth was dry from breathing hard. His jaw hurt from holding it so tight. A nearby coyote let out a long, slow howl. Lawrence saw in his mind a pack of coyotes coming upon him and tearing him apart. He dropped to his knees.

"Mom, Dad, I'm sorry," he cried out. "I'll never run away again. I'm scared! Help me!"

No one could hear him. Burying his head in his knees, he cried and cried. The tears made big wet spots on his pantlegs. After a while his eyes ran dry. He closed his eyes real tight, prayed fiercely, and then opened them, hoping he'd find himself at home. But when he opened them, there was only darkness, and he was still in the desert.

Turning his head, he made something out on the hillside. A light of some kind. He calmed himself and slowly got up and headed toward it. At first it appeared to be an electric light. As he got closer he saw that it was a campfire. He crept forward, making his way from tree to tree to keep hidden.

He eased down on his belly. The yellow flames shot straight up and the sparks went up further still and slipped into the night sky. He traveled the last thirty yards on his knees, feeling his way with his hands. Finally, he was just outside the circle of light. He got behind a tree and slowly separated the branches to take a look.

There was a blazing campfire around several rocks, and the wood was piled high on the bonfire. A coffeepot sat on a small rack above the fire and flames were racing up the sides. A giant hand suddenly came into view and reached down to draw the coffeepot out of the fire. A cup was thrust forward and coffee came pouring out. Lawrence was almost afraid to see what was at the end of that arm. He looked. It was the Indian—the one crossing the river that day.

When the Indian sat back against a rock, Lawrence could no longer see him, so he had to part the branches more and lean forward to see him again. His face was like the fire itself, all red from chin to forehead. His eyes were jet black. Suddenly, that great arm reached down and pulled some meat from the fire. It looked like rabbit on a stick. He took out a knife, a big hunting knife, and carved off a chunk. The smell wafted his way, into the trees. Lawrence swallowed hard. He was starving.

The man chewed slowly. When he finished, he put the rest of the meat near the fire. He cleaned the knife on his pant leg and then with a fierce and powerful thrust he turned and threw the knife into the dark and it disappeared. An instant later it hit something, something that sounded like wood. Lawrence peered into the dark to see what it could be, but could see nothing. He leaned forward more, forcing the branches even wider apart. And the branch broke with a loud crack.

Lawrence froze. He kept his eye on the Indian, ready to run if the man came at him. But he didn't move. He didn't turn. He didn't even look in Lawrence's direction. He just chewed the meat slowly, drank his coffee and stared into the fire. A short time later, the man got up and walked into the darkness, toward where he had thrown the knife.

He's got a cabin or something back there—that's what the knife hit—and now he's gone to bed, thought Lawrence. Then he noticed the meat still sitting there next to the fire, and even though he was afraid his hunger won out. He dashed into the campsite, grabbed the meat, and turned to run. An arm shot out of the darkness and seized him by the shirt. He tried to escape, but couldn't. Another arm wrapped around his neck. He squirmed but could not get free.

"Let me go, let me go," yelled Lawrence. The hands lifted him up. "Here's your stupid meat," yelled Lawrence, dropping it into the dirt. "Now let me go."

Saying nothing, the Indian man hoisted the boy over his shoulder and stalked away, into the black black night, moving slowly but with great power.

2

"Sit there," said the man. "I'll get you some food."

They were in a Forest Service cabin, the kind built every five miles or so to provide shelter to hikers and cross-country skiers during snowstorms and summer lightning. It was only eight feet by ten, and had no windows. The only way in or out was the door. The floor was dirt. The lamp had been placed on a square wooden table, in the middle of the room. It gave off a pungent smell of oil and smoked heavily because the wick was too thick.

Hanging on three wooden pegs were two shirts and a jean jacket. A leather belt lay across the top of three hooks. It had a silver buckle, which hung down. In the corner of the cabin were two bags, one filled with beans and one with rice. Four skinned rabbits dangled from rope cords. They looked grotesque in the dim light, and not appetizing at all, even as hungry as Lawrence was. Against the wall stood a sturdy pair of cowboy boots. On another small table the man had his toothbrush and soap, next to a bowl. There was no bathroom.

A gun stood upright in the corner—a shotgun. On the shelf next to the gun was an opened box of shells.

"You're obviously hungry," said the man, "or you wouldn't have tried to steal my dinner. I'm going outside to make a plate. Don't try to run."

Lawrence nodded. The man slipped out, carrying a steel plate and a mug. A few moments later he returned with a plate of rabbit, beans and rice in one hand and a steaming cup of coffee in the other. He put them down. "Do you drink coffee?" he asked. "I don't have anything else but water." Lawrence nodded again. "Good, now eat."

Lawrence hesitated only a moment, then dug in. He cleaned that plate and then another. While he ate, the Indian sat without speaking and watched. When Lawrence finished, he put down his fork and pushed the plate away. The huge arm reached for it. Looking at it Lawrence knew why he had not been able to get away from this man.

"Want more?"

"I'm full," Lawrence replied. The Indian sat down and lit a cigarette. The purple smoke curled up to the ceiling.

"What are you doing out here at night?" asked the man.

"Nothing," mumbled Lawrence, lowering his head.

"You must have been doing something. It's dangerous out here."

"Not really."

"Were you lost?"

"Kind of."

The man smoked his cigarette. "You're the boy I saw today."

"When did you see me today?" Lawrence asked.

"Today, by the river, I saw what those boys did to you," he said.

"You saw that?"

"I heard somebody calling out. I went over to see what was the matter—and saw those boys bothering you."

Lawrence lowered his head.

"I saw what they did to you. It was not nice. I would have come to help you if he had used that knife . . . but he didn't."

"The big one with the red hair, that's Tony—he had the knife."

The Indian reached down and pulled out the monster hunting knife and held it in front of Lawrence's face. He abruptly turned the knife down and plunged it into the table. The sound reverberated throughout the cabin. "It is not who has the knife, but what one does with it. Isn't that right, young man?" Lawrence nodded quickly, unable to speak. The Indian laughed.

"What, if I may ask—what are you doing here?" asked Lawrence.

"I am Dennis," he said, withdrawing the knife. "Dennis Yazzie. I'm a Navajo. I live near Shiprock, on the Navajo Nation. I come here once every six months and stay in this cabin for two weeks."

"What for?" asked Lawrence, gathering his courage.

Dennis reached over without a word and sprung the latches on the two black cases and opened them both with a great sweep of his arms. Even in the small yellowish light of the oil lamp, the room came alive with the glittering of silver. Great green and black stones popped up into the room, like great colorful icebergs of stone. The cases were full of gleaming silver jewelry with turquoise stones and mother of pearl. Navajo jewelry.

"It's . . . it's beautiful," said Lawrence, hovering over the shining objects. The room seemed to get warmer. The glimmering seemed to give off warmth.

"You made all this?" asked Lawrence.

"Yes, do you like it?"

"I sure do."

Dennis took a shiny turquoise stone out of one case. He held it up to the lamp. It was the size of a peach pit. Even in the dim light Lawrence could see its brilliant greenish-blue color, its black pockets, and rough surface. Yet in some places it was shiny and reflected light from the lamp.

"I want you to have this turquoise stone," said Dennis.

"You want to give it to me?"

"My father gave it to me when I was young. I was afraid then too. He told me it would help me be brave. It worked for me then, so now it will work for you."

"I don't want to be brave. I want to be strong. So that I can fight back when Tony comes for me."

"First be brave, then be strong."

Lawrence looked at the stone. "This will help me be brave?" asked Lawrence.

"If you believe in it. It has special powers. It will teach you not to be afraid. But be careful. Often it has unexpected consequences."

"Like what?"

"That you must see for yourself. Put it in your pocket and tomorrow when you go back to school perhaps you won't be afraid."

"I'm not going back."

Dennis smiled. "You might want to wait and see about that."

"All right," said Lawrence. "Thank you. It's very nice."

His stomach now full, Lawrence was growing tired. Dennis must have noticed, because he went to the corner and pulled out an Indian blanket and rolled it out on the dirt floor. "It's not much, but it's better than being out there with the coyotes. Sleep here." Dennis rolled up a shirt to use as a pillow. Lawrence fell into the bed and Dennis put another blanket on top.

Lawrence closed his eyes and started to float away. But something brought him back. What is that sound? he wondered. He opened his eyes just long enough to see Dennis holding a flute. Gentle music filled the cabin and his head. It was an Indian song, bright and happy and sad and full of longing. Lawrence closed his eyes.

He woke with a start. There were voices outside the cabin, calling out. Familiar voices.

"Hey, Larry Boy, come on out. Or we'll burn down your little cabin here, with you and your Indian buddy in it."

He dressed quickly. Dennis was still asleep. This was not his fight anyway. He crept to the door and opened it a crack. It was dawn. The sun was coming up over the hills. He didn't see anybody. So he ran for it.

"There he is!" yelled Tony, as he ran by. Digging his sneakers into the sand, Lawrence made his way to the top of a hill and stood surrounded by piñon trees. I'm too far into the desert, he thought. They're sure to catch me.

"I've got him!" yelled Frankie, racing up the side of the hill.

But Lawrence was off, running down the other side, skirting the long-armed cactus and the clumps of chamisa.

"Get him! Get him!" yelled Tony.

Tony's got that knife and he's going to kill me and bury me deep in the desert where no one will find me and he can get away with it, thought Lawrence.

A cactus caught his arm, tearing his shirt at the elbow and cutting him, but he didn't stop. He was running with everything he had, but they were gaining on him.

"Better give it up, Larry Boy," shouted Tony. "The more you run, the worse it's gonna be." The four boys were running in and out of the trees, closing the gap. A great rock barred his way, so Lawrence scrambled up it. Tony and the others gathered around the base of the rock.

"Larry Boy, you can't get away, so come on down now," said Tony.

"No," replied Lawrence.

"Then I'm coming up," said Tony, almost gleefully. He got his footing and started to climb. Lawrence couldn't escape down the backside of the rock. It was thirty feet down. He'd break his leg on the rocks below, surely. Lawrence thought, he'll be up here soon and he'll kill me with that knife and throw me off. I need a way out of this. Tony was already half way up the rock when Lawrence remembered the turquoise stone. Didn't Dennis say it would give him courage? Maybe it will work, after all, he thought. He took it out and held it and it grew warm in his hand. Then it grew so hot he could barely handle it.

"What do you want from me?" the stone asked him.

"I . . . I don't know," replied the boy, startled.

"You must tell me," replied the stone. "Tell me, and I will help you."

"I want to run away."

"No, that I cannot help you with. Tell me what you really want."

"Quick, he's almost here."

"You must think hard, Lawrence. What do you want?"

Lawrence could not think. What? What? What could it be?

Tony had now reached the top of the rock and the sight of his huge red head sent a jolt of fear through his body that stung right down to his toes. It almost sent him toppling off the rock, but the jolt shocked him into thinking.

"I don't want to be afraid," he said to the stone. "I don't want to be afraid of Tony ever again."

Lawrence jumped. Just as he left the rock, he felt Tony's powerful arms around his neck. They flew off into the air. He waited to hit the ground, but instead his vision went blurry and the world around him became a vast streak of color. Wind whipped wildly all around them as they fell. Lawrence opened his mouth to call out, but the wind pushed the words back in. The two boys fell, twisting in the air, endlessly falling, it seemed. Finally, Lawrence landed softly in some sand, Tony on top of him.

"Get off, get off!" he yelled. Tony rolled over.

"Oh, shut up, Larry, you're just lucky I'm not hurt. That was some fall, you know. We went off that rock there and—"

They both looked up at a huge rock cliff, soaring up as far as their eyes could see.

"It's gone," said Tony, suddenly quiet. "What happened?"

"I don't know."

"Where are we?"

"I don't know."

"Hey, this is your fault," said Tony. "You pulled me off that rock."

Lawrence ignored him and walked away from the cliff. Before them lay an endless barren valley surrounded by towering peaks rising straight out of the ground and going higher than they could see.

"There is something very strange going on here," said Lawrence.

"Oh, what a brain! Of course there's something going on here. We must have fallen down a hill or something."

"No, look."

Suddenly, the peaks began to move. The mountains—were moving! At first it was up and down, but then side to side. The ground shook, knocking the boys headfirst into the sand. As Lawrence looked up, a giant object was coming right for him from above, something huge and flat, about to crush him. He desperately tried to roll out of the way, but it fell right on him. Strangely, he found there were spaces on the bottom of the thing, whatever it was, just big enough to fit into. It became completely dark. A moment later it lifted off and Lawrence got up unharmed.

"What is it?" shouted Tony, running away.

Then another one just like the first appeared from nowhere. It created a huge explosion of dust as it landed not far from where Lawrence was standing. As the dust cleared, Lawrence could make out some lettering on it.

"Oh, my God," said Lawrence, staring dumbfounded.

"What? What?" yelled Tony.

"It's . . . no, it can't be," he whispered.

"What is it? What is it?"

"Read it—straight ahead."

Tony looked up. The letters read: N I K E.

"That . . . can't be."

"Here it comes," shouted Lawrence, running wildly.

As the sneaker landed, the tremendous force threw them to the ground again. A giant lace fell on top of Lawrence and without thinking he grabbed on. Tony grabbed it, too. A moment later it picked them up and flung them through the air. Lawrence let go and landed in a pile of soft sand. Tony fell not far away into a patch of grass. The mountains, Ron, Frankie, and Manny, moved off into the distance.

"Come back," yelled Tony, running after them. "Don't leave me here, don't leave me here. Come back! Come back!"

"They can't hear you," said Lawrence, calmly picking himself up.

Tony ran back and grabbed Lawrence. "What have you done?" Tony screamed. "Is this magic? What did you do?"

"I didn't do it," he replied quietly.

"This is some kind of trick. It makes us think we're the size of a bug, but it's all a trick, isn't it?" asked Tony desperately.

"It's not a trick."

"Then what?" yelled Tony.

"It's the stone."

"Stone? What stone?"

"Dennis gave it to me—"

"Who's Dennis?" demanded Tony.

"The Indian guy, from the cabin. He gave me a turquoise stone. He said it had strange powers. This must be what he meant."

"Give me the stone," said Tony.

Lawrence opened his hand, but the stone was gone. He checked his pockets, but no stone. He looked around him, but it was nowhere to be found. "I guess I lost it," he said.

"You lost it?"

"When we jumped off the rock, it got so hot in my hand that I had to let go," said Lawrence.

"So where is it?"

Lawrence shrugged. "It's out there, in the desert somewhere."

"Oh, that's just great, Larry Boy, just great."

"You see the top of that mountain?" replied Lawrence, pointing to the rock cliff. "That's where we jumped from. If I dropped it on the way down, it could be a two-day hike to find it—in any direction."

"What are you telling me? That we're stuck here? That we can't leave? That you lost the stone?"

"I guess so," said Lawrence calmly.

Tony's jaw started to shake, his lip quivered, and he burst out crying. "We're lost, lost, lost," he blubbered. "No one can find us, and we're sure to be eaten or stepped on."

"It'll be okay," said Lawrence, slumping down. "But we've got to think fast, or we'll be . . ."

"Eaten, or crushed, or torn apart—and it's your fault," yelled Tony.

A shadow came over them. At first Lawrence thought it was a just cloud blocking the sun, but there wasn't a cloud in the sky today. It was clear blue and completely cloudless. Tony turned around, shrieked and fell down. A hideous thing was coming for them, a giant creature with many hairy arms scampering in the dirt, a great round belly, two huge glassy eyes, and a stinger hanging down.

"I'm getting out of here," screamed Tony.

Its monstrous black eyes were bearing down on them as they ran. They came up over a small hill and ran around the back of a tree, but the spider was gaining. As they ran, Tony kept pushing Lawrence back to get ahead. A giant twig, still filled with berries from a piñon tree, loomed in their path and they both fell face-first over it. When they looked back, the spider was closing in.

"Quick, under here," said a rough voice.

They looked around. There was nothing.

"Under here. Under the bark. Can't you see anything? Quick, the brute is almost here. Dive for it."

Lawrence quickly bent down and saw under the bark a small opening. And in the opening was a pudgy white creature, round and fat with two dancing antennas.

The spider was almost upon them. Friend or foe—he couldn't tell. But they had to chance it. The two boys dove onto their bellies and scrambled under the bark. Tony shot forward and got safely away from the spider's legs, but Lawrence wasn't so lucky. The spider got a hold of his ankles.

"Tony, help me," yelled Lawrence. "Give me your hand. Pull me in."

Tony froze in fright.

"Come on, he's going to get me," Lawrence pleaded, stretching out his arm.

But Tony didn't move.

3

"Does your tail come off?" asked the white pudgy creature, its head tilted to one side.

"What?" stammered Lawrence, struggling to free himself.

"Can't you hear anything?" said the creature. "I said, does your tail come off? If it does, let it come off. It's your only chance, I'd say."

"Well, my tail doesn't come off," said Lawrence, quickly unhitching his pants and sliding them off, "but how's this?"

Too late the spider realized that he was shedding his skin and Lawrence slipped under the bark to safety. Furious at losing his meal, the spider paced around the tree. They could see his legs going back and forth.

"Oh, take off, fur mouth," yelled the white creature. "You can't eat everything in the territory. So beat it and don't come back."

All three huddled inside, staring at the bottoms of the black legs. Lawrence turned to look at their host. He had a long body, like a fat hot dog, with a large round belly, incredibly white skin, and whipping antennas.

"You're a termite," Lawrence blurted.

"Well, of course I'm a termite. What did you expect—the Queen of the Creenios?"

"The Creenios?" said Tony, stumbling over the word. "Who are they?"

The termite eyed them suspiciously, again tilting his head. "You don't know who the Creenios are? Where are you fellows from anyway?"

"Santa Fe," announced Tony.

"Never heard of it," replied the termite, dismissing it. "Must be another territory. You'll excuse me for a moment."

And with that, the termite turned, opened his mouth wide and took a terrific bite out of the wall. A loud crunching sound filled the chamber and a stream of liquid flowed out from the gash in the tree.

"Do you mind . . . I mean, could we have a taste?" asked Lawrence, eyeing the appealing liquid.

"Why, of course, be my guest."

Lawrence put his lips into the sticky water and drank and drank and drank.

"Hey, let me have some," said Tony, pulling him off.

Wiping his face dry on his sleeve, Lawrence turned to their new friend. "I'm Lawrence. Nice to meet you."

"I'm Gusteffes Mifores Terralus," said the termite, "at your service. And just who would this be?" He furrowed his brow.

"That's my friend Tony."

"I'm not your friend," said Tony. "I hate your guts and you're gonna pay for this, Larry boy, you got that? I'm going to be going my own way now. No sense hanging around with a loser like you."

"Shouldn't we stay together?" asked Lawrence, dumbfounded.

"I don't need you," said Tony. "You'll just slow me down. I'm gonna go find that turquoise stone and get outta here. And I'm not waiting around for you, Larry boy. So see ya."

He slipped out on his belly, looked this way and that, and then scrambled to his feet and was gone.

"Tony, Tony, come back, we have to stay together," Lawrence yelled after him. "Tony!" But he was gone. Lawrence leaned back against the wall, closed his eyes, and tried not to cry.

"Well, what of it, my fellow? So he's off." Gusteffes shrugged. "I wouldn't make too much of it. He wasn't much of a good fellow anyway. And, besides, he's not much of a friend if he wouldn't help you when the spider had you. He would have let you die."

"If he finds the stone first, he'll leave me here forever."

"But if you find the stone first? What then?"

"Oh, I don't know . . . I guess it doesn't matter now anyway, because I'll never make it out there alone."

"Well, well, we'll see about that," said Gusteffes. "Stand up and let's take a look at you." Lawrence stood. "Turn, turn, let's see your backside. Remarkable! How do you defend yourself?"

"With these, I guess," said Lawrence, holding up his arms, which felt puny and ridiculous at the moment.

"Any poison sacks?"

"No."

"Do you have sharp teeth at least—for killing?"

"I'm afraid not. We just use them for eating."

"How very strange, how very remarkable," said the termite. "It's a wonder your species has survived at all. But hold on, I may be able to help."

Gusteffes went to work immediately, tearing off a huge chunk of wood from the tree and working at it furiously. After several minutes a long pointy object began to take shape. "It's a sword," shouted Lawrence, gleefully.

"I don't know what you call it," said Gusteffes, sharpening the point, "but it will work like a stinger, though with no poison, I'm afraid.

"It's wonderful," said Lawrence, taking it and swiping at the air. It felt good in his hands, crude as it was. But a moment later, he slumped against the wall.

"What is it now?" asked Gusteffes, waddling over to him.

"Oh, I'm very appreciative, really I am, but even with this, I don't think I'll last a day out there."

"I think you'll do just fine."

"In case you haven't noticed, Gusteffes, I have no food, no water, no place to live, no nothing."

"On the contrary, my funny looking fellow, you have the very two things that you need to survive in the desert," said Gusteffes. "You have the stinger I gave you and you have your brain. I could tell that right away. You are smarter than most out here, and certainly smarter than your friend that just left. Use your brain and you will survive!"

Just then there were scuffling sounds and voices coming from deep inside the tree. Gusteffes cocked his head for a moment to listen, then motioned to Lawrence. "Oh, you must go, you must go now, yes yes yes, absolutely, be off before my sisters come and want to eat you."

"But I was hoping to stay here, with you, at least for one night," pleaded Lawrence.

"Impossible. My fellow termites would want to feast on you for certain. They are not as open minded as I am."

"But where shall I go?"

"Find protection—with the other creatures of the desert. Think of only one thing—survival! Now be off with you."

Lawrence nodded reluctantly.

"All right, but thank you," he said, and slowly slid out into the sunlight. His eyes hurt after being in the dim light. He found his pants where the spider had abandoned them and quickly pulled them on.

"And one other thing," said Gusteffes, sticking out his head once again. "Beware of Antentius."

"Who's Antentius?" Lawrence asked, turning.

But the termite was gone.

Lawrence was alone outside the tree. Tony was nowhere in sight. Slowly, he started to walk. The walking was difficult because the sand granules were as big as softballs under his feet, but he soon got used to it. He didn't know where he was going, but he just kept on. It'll be dark soon, he thought. I have to find a place to sleep or I'll die in the night. So he kept walking. The trees around him were as high as skyscrapers; the sticks he ran into were as big as redwood trees. The hills looked like the highest mountain peaks.

The afternoon sun was burning. He tried to cover the back of his neck with his hands but it was hard to walk that way for long. His wounds began to hurt. He saw a great inviting shady area under a piñon tree, but kept moving because it provided no shelter. "I hope Tony hasn't found the turquoise stone and left me here," he said aloud.

He spotted a petal from a cactus flower, a single purple petal that was the richest purple he had ever seen. It smelled like the most wonderful perfume in the world. It had settled against a rock. Lawrence climbed up and used the flower petal as a slide. It was a glorious ride; it felt like he was flying. He climbed up and slid down again and again. "Why, being here isn't so bad," he thought.

But his driving thirst suddenly put an end to his play. It had been hours since that drink in Gusteffes's tree. He went in search of water, and found in a clearing a huge red ball, ten times bigger than he was. Lawrence approached carefully, step by step. He slowly reached out and touched it. The skin was rough, but it was also soft when he pushed against it.

He backed off twenty paces, withdrew the sword tucked neatly under his belt, and ran forward. The sword pierced the skin with a swishing sound and a wave of red liquid, more like syrup, oozed out all around him. He bent down and took a taste. It was sweet. It's a berry, he thought, a juniper berry. He splashed in it for a few minutes and then started pulling at the berry meat. It tasted better than anything he had ever eaten in his life. With his sword he cut large pieces off and ate them with both hands. His arms were covered in syrup, but he didn't care. He just kept eating the meat and drinking the liquid.

When he was done, he wiped the syrup off as best he could. Then he collapsed against the side of the giant fruit. I should go look for the stone, he thought. But I'll just . . . rest . . . here . . . for . . . a . . . while. And with that, he fell asleep in the shade of the berry.

"Aaaaaaaa!"

A sharp pain woke him. His eyes flew open and there was a monstrous red face staring directly into his. He looked one way and then another. Lots of red faces, huge and grotesque. His arms were pinned to the berry by the legs of these creatures and he could not move, no matter how much he struggled to free himself.

"What is it?" said one of the creatures, inspecting Lawrence.

"I've never seen anything like it," said another. "Have you?"

"Of course I have," said a third. "It's a kind of spider . . . I think."

"This is not a spider, you night rodent," said the first. "It's not from the territory, if you ask me. Kill it and let's move on."

"Let's get Antentius," said a creature. "He'll know what to do."

Antentius? *Antentius?* Did he say that name? Wasn't that the name Gusteffes had warned him against? It was, he was sure. Lawrence struggled even harder to get away, but the many legs held him fast. Lawrence took a closer look at his captors. He could make out swirling antennas, giant compound eyes cut like thousands of small jewels, tiny hairs just above the mouths, and the ferocious jaw-like things that came out from the head and snapped just a short distance from his face.

Ants! Red ants! One ant turned and then Lawrence could see the muscular abdomen, where all three pairs of legs came out; the waist, which connected to the back end of the ant; and finally the gaster, the puffy large hind quarters which housed the stinger and the poison. One sting from that I'll be dead, he thought, looking at it with dread.

"What do we have here? Is this a Magyar trick?" boomed a voice.

A monster ant, twice as big as the others, approached. He had massive eyes that flitted this way and that. His face was so large and hideous Lawrence almost got sick. He leaned in and put his face right up to Lawrence's, so that he could smell his stinky breath.

"We found him asleep next to this berry," said one guard.

"Why, never in my life," said Antentius, clearly astonished. "What is it?"

"It's a spider, I think," said a guard.

"It's not a spider, " said Antentius.

"Right, it's definitely not a spider," said the guards in unison.

"Could be a kind of moth," said Antentius.

"Yes, a moth! It's a moth," said the guards.

"No, it's got no wings," said Antentius.

"Can't be a moth," said the guards.

"Is it a termite?"

"A termite! A termite! Yes, of course."

"No, there's no antennas," said Antentius.

"No, not a termite, definitely not a termite."

"Scrawny little beast, isn't it?" he said, poking the boy. The guards crowded around. "All right, I give up, so just hold the little beast down. I'm going to chew him up. I'll take the liquid back to Queen Natoria. She loves new foods. Hold him so I can get my stinger on him."

"Not so fast, Antentius," a voice called out from the ridge. Antentius instantly unfastened his mandibles from Lawrence and turned. There on the ridge a hundred or more black ants were crowding the edge.

"Those Magyars are always trying to spoil my fun," seethed Antentius.

The red ants spread out, preparing for battle. "We're in their territory," said a guard quietly to Antentius.

"Yes . . ." replied Antentius, peering at the enemy. "I'm well aware of that. We're deep in their territory and they'll fight to the death. Even Magyars will do that on their own territory, cowards that they are."

The red ants—and Lawrence—were at the bottom of a rock bowl filled with sand. The black ants had the superior position on higher ground. Their leader stepped forward.

"That prey belongs to the Magyars," he said. "You're in our territory, you know the rules."

"Well, if it isn't Homeron and his miserable band of stink bugs," Antentius responded.

"Watch who you're calling a stink bug," called a tiny voice. It came from an ant so small that Lawrence could barely see the little thing.

"Oh, and you brought the runt—how kind and gentle you Magyars are," said Antentius. "That's why you'll lose the war."

"We don't kill our runts outright, if that's what you mean," said another voice, a softer female voice. "We see no reason to."

"If you pull back now, you will not be harmed," said the leader Homeron. "Otherwise we attack."

"They have us outnumbered ten to one," whispered the guard to Antentius.

"Antentius, the rules of the territory are clear," said Homeron. "Depart the battlefield and leave us the prey."

Antentius stalked toward the black ants. Lawrence could not help but admire the red ant's courage, to walk toward them fearlessly. He stood in the center of the sandy bowl, sneering at his enemies.

"You Magyars are a weak lot," said Antentius. "This is not your territory. This is Creenio territory now. This is my territory. You might as well take your little runt and hightail it back to your sickly queen and leave us soldiers to do our work."

The response was swift. "Attack!" ordered Homeron.

Black ants poured down from the ridge, and both sides reared back on their hind legs and charged. The reds were bigger and stronger, but the black ants were faster and struck like lightning. The reds fought with great fierceness, but could not match the larger forces. The reds sprayed poison on their enemies. The black ants used their stingers to kill the reds.

Antentius himself killed twenty black ants, ripping most apart with his mandibles. Then he gave the order to fall back.

"I want the foreigner," said Antentius. "Get him. Kill him quickly. We can carry him with us." They went for him but Lawrence saw them coming and ran up the side of the rock bowl, out of their reach.

The red ants quickly abandoned the battlefield, but one black ant pursued Antentius up the slope, without waiting for the others. Antentius quickly turned and seized him. He picked the soldier up in his massive mandibles and held him outstretched. The black soldier struggled but could not free himself.

"Let him go," ordered Homeron.

"You talk about rules," replied Antentius. "These are my rules." He cracked the black ant in two and dug his jaws into the body. The loud crunching sound filled the sandy bowl. The black ants, too far away to do anything, watched helplessly as their soldier was sucked dry and Antentius spit the shell out. Then he threw the carcass aside.

"Ah, I love the taste of Magyars," he said contentedly. "Soon I'll be feasting on the lot of you."

"You're lucky I'm in a good mood," said the tiny black runt, which had climbed up on Homeron's head. "Or I'd come up there and crack you in two."

Ignoring the runt, Antentius shouted, "This may be your territory now, but you can't hold it for long, and you know it. We Creenios are stronger and you Magyars are growing weaker every day. It won't be long before I'm feasting on your beloved Queen Andulusia, and I'll keep you all alive long enough to watch." Antentius threw his head back and laughed. Then he turned and with his soldiers scampered up the slope and disappeared.

"You know, I'd say he's got a real attitude problem," said the runt.

The black ants immediately filled the bowl, crowding around Lawrence. They poked and prodded and examined his limbs and jabbered away heatedly about him. He stood quietly and allowed them a thorough examination, raising his arms when they asked, showing them the inside of his mouth, even jumping up and down. He submitted to every request, until they had satisfied their curiosity.

What had Gusteffes told him: *Use your brain, and survive!*

"Who are you?" demanded Homeron.

"My name is Lawrence Bell."

"Where do you come from?"

"Another territory."

"What are you doing here?"

"I . . . I have come to help you fight the red ants," replied Lawrence confidently, though the thought came out of nowhere.

There was a murmuring of low voices behind Homeron. "Silence!" he yelled. "All right, we'll take you back to the queen. She can decide. Get ready to march."

4

"I've got to keep up."

The ants were moving rapidly through the chamisa bushes and Lawrence, near the end of the long line, was falling back. The ants scurried easily over rocks and through sand and over logs. They could go straight up things, using the suction cups on the end of their legs. But Lawrence had to go around everything. The line of ants suddenly headed down into a ravine. Scrambling to keep up, Lawrence was breathing hard when he finally got back in place.

Homeron was in command, but the female Sephea gave the orders. The ants followed her commands instantly. Lawrence decided to take a position near her, so he mustered all his strength and ran up behind her. She turned, seemed about to say something, thought better of it, and resumed her steady march. The landscape soon grew dim as the sun dropped behind Atalaya Ridge. The gullies darkened and the color went out of the desert in no time. Now it was even harder for

Lawrence to keep up. He stumbled and fell and skinned both knees.

As he picked himself up, he saw the head of the runt pop up over Sephea's shoulder. He made eye contact with him, but then disappeared. But a moment later he appeared again, and this time came and stood on Sephea's shoulder.

"Hiya!" he said.

He was sure funny looking, only about a tenth of the size of the others. Yet he seemed perfectly proportioned—just small. He had tiny antennas, a little bobbing head, stumpy little legs, a puffy abdomen, and a cute little gaster.

"Hi," replied Lawrence. This little ant made him smile immediately.

"You're a strange looking fellow," said the runt.

"So I've been told," replied Lawrence.

"Well, in case you haven't noticed, I'm not the best looking berry on the tree either. I'm Bleato. Nice to meet you." His voice was squeaky high, but not unpleasant to the ear.

"Same here," replied Lawrence.

"I'm the runt of the colony. You know what that is?"

"I have a pretty good idea."

"You might as well know the history. Every five or six generations the colony gets one," said Bleato. "The egg pops open and whattaya got—a very tiny ant. That's me. The job comes with a lot of abuse, but hey, we all got problems, right?"

"Yes, I think so."

Bleato leaned forward and whispered, "The only real problem is that they won't let me be a soldier."

"Why not?" asked Lawrence.

"They think I'd disgrace the colony, on account of my size. So I get to go on journeys, foraging, that kind of thing, the boring stuff, but not fighting. They won't let me kill a Creenio. And to die without killing a Creenio is not to have lived at all, if you ask me."

"I see."

"The soldiers keep me around for entertainment value, so I play along, make jokes, that kind of thing—"

"That's enough, Bleato," scolded Sephea. "Don't talk to the foreigner."

Bleato winked at Lawrence and lowered his voice. "All right, so tell me about you. What brings you to our territory, you dashing foreigner type?"

"Oh, there's not much to tell. I—"

"You know there's a prophecy in Magyar Hill that a foreigner will come out of the hills and save the colony," said Bleato. "That could be you."

"I hardly think so," replied Lawrence. "I just want to keep up."

"Bleato, I said no more talking!"

"Okay, okay, but Seph, there's something I think you ought to know."

"What is it?"

"Big rainstorm coming. Big, very big."

"Bleato, the sky is clear."

"Seph, we're talking big here, not puny like me, but big, colossal, huge, the mother of all storms, the queen of all storms, I mean rain."

Sephea sighed. "All right, I'll tell Homeron." She moved swiftly ahead of the others to find their leader.

"How do you know that it's going to rain?" asked Lawrence.

Bleato shrugged. "I get this thing in my neck, and I can't turn it and yow it hurts so much, and. . . ."

Storm clouds appeared a short time later, just as Bleato had predicted. It started to rain.

"What did I tell you?" Bleato gloated. "What did I tell you!"

"You were right," yelled Lawrence, over the storm.

The rain got heavy. Raindrops the size of buckets of water hit Lawrence in the back and on the head again and again. He got completely drenched in seconds. It got so dark he couldn't see his own feet. The others were only dark shapes ahead.

"Hey, hey, hey, where are you going?" yelled Bleato.

Lawrence stopped cold. "I don't know. I'm just walking."

"You're at the edge of a cliff. One more step and you'd be spider food at the bottom of the ravine. Can't you see?"

"Not really."

"All right, I'll ride on your shoulder and tell you where to go."

Bleato climbed up. Suddenly, there was a giant thunderclap followed by a tremendous bolt of lightning. It lit up the desert floor for one spectacular moment. They were standing on top of a cliff overlooking the colony—a great mound of sand below. He had seen anthills when he walked in the desert, but this one loomed like a coliseum. A torrent of water was rushing down the ravine, and only a slim retaining wall kept the water from hitting the colony head on. The light faded.

"We have to warn the queen," said Homeron. "Come on."

"Let's move it out," yelled Bleato. Lawrence was almost blind again, and to get down that cliff he needed Bleato sitting on his shoulder and shouting commands.

"Stop. Go that way, no that way, good, good, now two steps the other way. There's a rock, be careful. Watch out for the hole. Hold that root. Good, good. Big step down. Not bad. Keep going."

Soon they were on solid ground, and he could hear the sand crunching under his feet. "Nice going, you made it down the cliff," yelled Bleato over the storm, as they approached the colony.

At the entrance, Lawrence froze. What am I doing? he said to himself. I can't go into an ant colony! *An ant colony!*

"Hey, who's holding things up?" yelled Homeron from behind.

"Uh, you better go now," said Bleato hurriedly. "You don't want to get his bigness angry."

But Lawrence could not move. Turn and run, he thought, just run, they'll never come after me in this storm. Their colony is about to flood, so they won't care about me. I'll just run off into the desert. But then what? *Think and survive.* Isn't that what Gusteffes said? *Find protection.* I have to find protection, but what if they just tear me apart down there? There will be thousands of ants down there, and me in the middle of them all. God help me.

"Hey, get this line moving!"

"Uh, excuse me, but you've got a few hundred soldiers behind you in the rain, waiting to get in, and you're blocking the entrance," said Bleato. "Is this some kind of foreigner thing or what?"

"Get moving!" yelled Sephea.

He made a decision and bolted forward. Down, down they went, into the colony. At first he could see nothing, and Bleato had to tell him when to turn and when to duck, but then something in the tunnel walls began to glow greenish-yellow. It got brighter and brighter.

"I can see," he yelled to Bleato. "I can see. There's something glowing in the rock."

Suddenly, they came out into a massive chamber filled with tens of thousands of ants crawling all over each other. In the center of the chamber, two giant ants were fighting. Bleato quickly led Lawrence up a pile of ants where they could take a look. Several ants turned and looked at him as they passed, but then went back to watching the combat. The spectators waved their antennas madly and yelled and spit and snapped their jaws. It was like a boxing match, with two oversized ants battling it out.

"That's our queen there, Andulusia," said Bleato, pointing to one of the combatants. "She's a tough old bird but she's been getting beat on for a long time."

"What's happening?" asked Lawrence.

"There are two queens in our colony right now," said Bleato. "Sometimes we got five, sometimes one. Right now we got two. Everyone is loyal to one or the other. Our queen is Andulusia and their queen is Meetrio."

"Why are they fighting?" Lawrence asked.

"Meetrio wants to rule alone. So it's a fight to the death, our queen versus their queen. Winner take all. One queen will rule, the other gets fed to the spiders."

"What happens to you if your queen loses?"

"Oh, nothing much. Just humiliation, exile, and death. That's all."

"You die?" exclaimed Lawrence.

"Yeah, they kill most of us and put the rest out of the colony for the woodpeckers to pick us off."

"You seem so calm about it?"

"It's the law of the colony. I'm just a runt, so what do you want me to do about it? But you're with me, so it's your neck too. So root for Andulusia, if you know what's good for you."

"Right. Go, Andulusia," shouted Lawrence.

"It's Queen Andulusia, tarantula brain," said Bleato.

"Oh, sorry."

Down below, Queen Meetrio lunged forward and clamped her mandibles on Andulusia's front leg. She fell to one side to keep her leg from being broken in two. With Andulusia on her side, Meetrio, a monstrous figure in the green light, straddled her opponent and prepared to sting. But Andulusia threw her off just in time and rolled over, rising and locking mandibles with her once again.

The two queens circled each other slowly, their antennas swirling over great eyes that looked like a thousand cut jewels. One lunged, then the other. Meetrio ripped at her adversary and twice opened wounds. Andulusia, losing ground, gambled and reared up on her hind legs and lunged at Meetrio, snapping her jaws. Meetrio had to retreat, but soon struck back.

Meetrio grabbed her opponent from below, in the abdomen, and yanked. Andulusia tumbled forward and Meetrio seized her and drove her jaws into the soft underbelly. Andulusia cried out in pain. It looked like the end was near. But with one great thrust, Andulusia threw off her opponent, rose to her feet, and locked antennas. The great queens slowly circled each other and then, surprisingly, they bowed to each other and left the arena.

"Who won?" asked Lawrence.

"No one yet," replied Bleato. "They keep fighting, day after day. But Queenie's gonna have to do better than that," said Bleato. "We got lucky today, but tomorrow, who knows. . . ." He shrugged.

"Come, we must alert the queen," said Homeron.

"She doesn't need any warning," said Bleato. "She knows she's getting her gaster kicked out there."

"About the flood, Bleato," Sephea said, losing patience.

"Oh, yeah, the flood. Forgot about that."

The tunnels were clogged with soldiers and nurses and hunters and gatherers, all making their way back to their chambers. It was slow going for their party, even though Homeron called out that they had an urgent message for the queen. "Those hunter-gatherers are so stupid," said Bleato.

When at last they pushed their way into the queen's antechamber, they found chaos. The court was in an uproar. Courtiers were bumping each other, letting their antennas swirl, and chattering non-stop, mostly about how the queen could not hold out much longer.

"Stand aside," yelled Homeron. "Important message for the queen."

"Wait in line with the rest of us," yelled a member of the court. "We all want to see the queen."

"This is a matter concerning the survival of the colony."

"Oh, Homeron, just what is it?" said an ant, approaching. "Can't you see we're in the middle of a real tizzy. The queen needs a rubdown, the court is spinning out of control, and we fight again tomorrow. We're swamped up here."

"I have to see the queen."

"Unless you have a message from Queen Meetrio that she wants to step down, forget it."

"Take me to her, Naxas, or I'll have you on guard duty at the Creenio border by this time tomorrow."

"Why didn't you say so in the first place? Follow me."

"Who is that?" Lawrence whispered to Bleato.

"Oh, that's Nervous Naxas, personal courtier to the queen. He's the guy you talk to when you need to see the queen. But he's always in a total snit about things."

The court members were bouncing off the walls and into each other, and they had a hard time getting through. Finally, they reached the queen's chamber and went in.

"All stand for Her Highness, Queen Andulusia," shouted Naxas.

"We are standing, you idiot," said Bleato.

"Oh, so you are. Well, no matter." He approached the queen. "Your majesty, are you willing to take a report from Homeron? Some news about the survival of the colony, or something like that. . . ."

Lawrence could not take his eyes off the queen. She had a shapely look, a massive head, a huge belly, tremendous eyes, and amazingly long legs. But what really captivated Lawrence was her face, especially her smile. It was a smile of immense nobility. She seemed worn out but serene. Her expression, even in exhaustion, was one of steadiness and grace. He liked her right away, without even knowing her.

"Homeron, come forward," she said, and her voice was fine and sure. He approached and bowed his head to the floor.

"Rise and give your report," said the queen.

"I regret to inform your majesty that I have made an inspection of the ridge overlooking the colony," said Homeron. "There is a great storm above. In my opinion, the colony will flood—and soon."

This news sent the court into pandemonium. There was more running about and bumping into each other and hysterical chattering. But then, the queen raised her foreleg and the room was instantly quiet.

"Is it still raining?" asked the queen, calmly.

"Yes, your majesty," said Homeron. "The ridge has worn away to little more than the width of my leg. The water will soon break through."

"And what do you propose that we do?" asked the queen, lowering her head.

"We must evacuate the colony immediately and move to higher ground."

This suggestion set off tremendous bobbing of heads and murmuring and antennas swirling.

"Silence, please," said the queen, a little sterner this time. "Naxas, go to Queen Meetrio without delay. Tell her we must remove ourselves from the colony at our earliest possibility."

"But-but-but-but. . . ."

"Don't prattle," intoned the queen. "There might not be much time."

"All right, I will go," said Naxas, "but Meetrio will think it's a trick."

"She may, but impress upon her that this is not about our combat, but about the sake of the entire colony."

"She'll think we're afraid to continue fighting and are looking for a delay."

The queen was unfazed by his words, as if anticipating them. "Then use your powers to persuade Meetrio," she said. "If you fail in this, the colony may not survive."

"Oh, my, not survive, not survive—then I have to tell her, don't I? Yes, I will, I'll be very firm. Queen Meetrio, I'll say, hear this and hear it good . . ." he said as he disappeared down the tunnel.

A buzz swept through the chamber. Members of the court now turned their attention to the foreigner. They looked and pointed and jabbered to themselves. Lawrence grew frightened.

"Now, Homeron," said the queen, "I see you have brought a visitor to our colony. Are there not rules against bringing foreigners into our colony?"

"There are, your majesty."

"Kill him, kill him, kill him," the court started to chant.

"We found him while on patrol," continued Homeron. "Antentius had him and was about to carry him off. We fought a skirmish and beat the Creenios back. I brought the foreigner back . . . well, I brought him back because he said he had come to help us fight the Creenios."

"The prophecy, the prophecy," murmured the members of the court.

"Unless he can save us from the rain, I do not see how his services could be put to use," said the queen.

"If your majesty orders, I shall have him chewed and the liquid sent to the nursery," said a guard.

"Oh, you guards think of nothing but killing, killing, killing," Bleato interrupted. "Doesn't that get a little old? Why not throw him off Rockface Cliff first? That'll be tremendous fun for all you guards."

"Bleato, not now," said the queen.

"I was just trying to help, your maj—after all, we have to think about the prophecy, don't we?'

"I think I can handle this," the queen said. Turning her soft gaze to Lawrence, she said, "Approach."

Lawrence slowly walked up to the queen and stood motionless. There was a long awkward silence while she looked him over. All eyes were upon him. His legs started to wobble and his mouth went dry.

"Pssst, kneel down, termite head," whispered Bleato.

"Oh." Lawrence bowed his head to the floor.

"You may rise," said the queen. "So you say you are here to help us fight the Creenios?"

Lawrence nodded. "Yes . . . your majesty."

Bleato cut in. "If you ask me, the Creenios are quaking right now. Just look at him! What a specimen!"

"And just how will you fight for us?" asked the queen. "You have no long legs, no jaws, no sharp teeth, no mandibles, no poison sack, no stinger. What do you have to fight the Creenios?"

"I have this," Lawrence said, pulling out the crude sword and holding it over his head. For a moment the court was silent. Then the room erupted in laughter. Even the queen could not stop from chuckling. Embarrassed, Lawrence lowered his sword and stood there feeling miserable. I'm no use to them, he thought. Now they will kill me.

"I'm afraid we don't allow foreigners in our colony," said the queen, when the laughter died down. "However, you have come with good intentions. You shall not be killed but taken out of the colony and left."

Just at that moment Naxas burst out of the tunnel and collapsed in front of the queen, gasping for air. "I . . . I . . . I have run all the way from Queen Meetrio's chambers, and . . . and . . . and. . . ."

"And what?" asked the queen.

"She says 'Nonsense!' That's what she said to me when I told her about the flood. 'Nonsense!' And she said if I come back she'll have me chewed up."

"What was her reason?" asked the queen.

"She said, she said, oh I can't say it. . . ."

"You may continue," ordered the queen.

"She said, 'Tomorrow I will kill Andulusia and you will all die with her. We are not leaving the colony.'"

"I see." The queen thought for a few moments. No one dared disturb her. Then, she spoke, looking down. "Naxas, go back to her. . . ."

"Oh, I couldn't, I couldn't, they'll chew me up, chew me," he replied.

"Go back," interrupted the queen, "and tell Meetrio that for the good of the colony I shall abdicate as soon as we reach higher ground."

The court was stunned. Naxas took a stumbling step toward her. "Your majesty, but that would mean, that would mean, that would mean death!"

"For the survival of the colony, we must sacrifice," she said calmly. "It is the only thing to do."

Suddenly, the ground started to shake and a low rumbling noise reverberated in the chamber. They all stopped to listen. The queen quickly stood up, sensing danger. The noise got louder and louder and the shaking became worse. No one moved. Then, the rumbling became a roar. The guards instinctively surrounded the queen, to protect her. But suddenly, all was silent. A moment later a blast of water came rushing out of the main tunnel and gushed into the chamber.

"The flooding has begun," shouted Homeron. "Long live the Queen."

5

"We'll make our stand in the egg-laying chamber," shouted Homeron, as he hustled the queen and the others into the tunnel. "We need to build a wall before the water gets there."

The tunnel abruptly opened into a chamber already half-filled with water pouring in from another tunnel. The opening to the egg-laying chamber, higher up, was still dry, but it was directly across the chamber, and the water was growing deeper by the second. The queen and her guards stood motionless.

"We have to get across," shouted Homeron.

"But how?" asked Sephea.

"I'm afraid I'm not accustomed to water travel," said the queen, calmly.

"What do we do?" shouted Sephea over the noise of the water.

"I'll show you," shouted Lawrence. The ants stared as he pulled off his shoes, knotted the laces and put them around his neck. Then he jumped into the water and did a strong crawl around the rapidly filling chamber. Then he swam back to the astonished ants.

"It's nothing really," said Lawrence. "Back home, we all do it."

"The queen goes first," ordered Homeron, as he placed her carefully on Lawrence's back and shoulders.

"Hold on, your majesty," said Lawrence, setting off. She was heavier than he had thought she would be, and he started to go under. He started to panic. What if I can't hold her and the queen drowns? he said to himself. They'll kill me for sure. But he found his stroke and quickly made it to the other side. Nurses from the egg-laying room were waiting and whisked the queen up the tunnel into the dry chamber. Lawrence made several trips, back and forth, taking several ants at a time. On his last lap, the water level reached the tunnel, and the last ants, along with Lawrence, scrambled up into the egg-laying room.

Homeron was already busy with his guards, building the wall. He hurried the last of them through the opening and sealed the wall. "I just hope it holds until the rain stops," he said. The queen came down to inspect their work. On the way back to her chamber, she passed Lawrence putting the finishing touches on the wall. She paused for a moment and smiled at him. That made him work even harder.

"Will it be strong enough?" Sephea whispered.

"I hope so," replied Homeron.

"Listen," said a guard. "The water has reached the wall."

"Your majesty, this wall may give way," said Homeron. "You should—"

"I'll stay," she said firmly. "But thank you anyway."

There was no more talk about it. Everyone was silent and stared at the wall. Several guards threw themselves against it to support it. If that wall gives way, we die, Lawrence suddenly realized. There's no place else to go. Suddenly, water spouted out of a hole. The guards stepped in quickly, and several drowned plugging the hole. It was awful for Lawrence to see them die, but the others didn't seem to be affected. Another hole opened up. Then another.

"I can feel the wall giving way," said one guard on the wall, pressing his body against the dirt.

"I can't hold it back," yelled another guard.

"Everyone, together—push!" yelled Homeron, throwing his body into the wall. Lawrence took his place next to Sephea, burying his shoulder into the wall.

"No need to fear," squeaked Bleato. "I've got my body on it now."

"That's very reassuring," replied Sephea.

"I think it's holding," said Homeron. Everyone listened, motionless.

"Yes, it's holding," said Sephea. They stepped back.

"But for how long?" said Homeron.

"And how long can we last without air?" asked Bleato, not really wanting an answer.

"We've been a colony for five thousand generations, and there have been floods before," said the queen, rising and heading up the tunnel. "There will be survivors."

Then, the waiting began. Homeron arranged several groups to take turns on the wall, holding it back, checking for leaks. As the guard changed, one ant at a time would be dispatched, so that the wall would not crumble. Lawrence was relieved of his post by a soldier. His shoulder hurt from pressing against the dirt. The only sounds were from tunnels below and above them filling up with water.

"I'm thirsty," said Bleato. "Can you believe it? The colony is filling with water and we've got nothing to drink. And I finished my crop long ago."

"What's a crop?" asked Lawrence.

"It's where we keep our food till later," he replied. "We chew it and then store it for late night snacks. I ate mine already."

Hours passed, and the wall held. Lawrence and Bleato took several turns on the wall. All was quiet outside.

"Do you think anybody else is alive?" asked Sephea.

The queen came back to see how things were going. There was no reason to wait in her chamber above, she told them, because if the wall broke her chamber would be flooded instantly. Hours went by and the air started to run out. Lawrence especially was having trouble breathing. Some ants passed out and fell off the wall. Others were too weak to take their places.

"Too much water and not enough air," said Bleato, coughing. "Usually it's the other way around in the desert. Funny."

The queen slumped on her back against the wall, in a very undignified pose, but no one had the strength to tend to her, not even her ladies-in-waiting. The guards, one by one, fell off the wall, until no one was supporting it. Homeron passed out. The queen passed out. Most of the guards went unconscious. Summoning all her strength, Sephea struggled to her feet and kicked the guards closest to the wall.

"Break down the wall," she said to the astonished guards.

"But what if. . . ." said one guard.

"If we don't we're going to die anyway," she gasped.

Lawrence lay on his side watching, too weak to get up and help. Sephea threw several soldiers aside and started clawing

at the earth herself. Spurred by her activity, the others joined in. With their mandibles they took away grain after grain of sand. Finally, Sephea punched through.

"I'm on the other side," she yelled. Those not passed out looked up in horror, expecting a gush of water. Instead there was a blast of fresh air. Sephea slumped against the wall and took several deep breaths, trying to keep her legs from wobbling.

"Nice going, Seph," said Bleato, breathing deep at the entrance.

Soon the fresh air revived all the ants.

"Look," said Homeron, pointing to some soldiers coming up the tunnel. "We're not the only survivors."

"Is Queen Andulusia alive?" called out the soldiers.

"Yes, she is safe," replied Homeron.

"Queen Meetrio is dead, drowned by the flood," reported the soldiers. "Long live the queen."

"Long live the Queen," said Bleato.

Queen Andulusia bowed her head. "She wanted me dead, I know," she said. "But she was a great queen and I shall miss her."

"Yeah, we're all real sorry she had to check out," said Bleato.

"You are the only queen now," said Homeron. "What shall we do with Meetrio's followers?"

"Leave them," said the queen. "There will be no killing and no exile. We have lost many, and we will not lose more. Let us turn our anger on the Creenios, who will try to take advantage of our weakness."

"I will go to the surface and see to our defenses," said Homeron.

"Yes," said the queen, "take charge of the army. Protect the colony."

"Yes, your majesty," he replied.

"Oh, and take the foreigner with you," said the queen. "I have decided that he may stay."

Bleato could not contain himself. "Queenie, you're the greatest," he called out.

Suddenly, Naxas stumbled into the chamber. "I must have fainted," he said. "What happened?"

"Just a bit of water," said the queen. "We're glad to have you with us, good Naxas."

"Sure, he's the life of the party," whispered Bleato.

"Lawrence, come forward," commanded the queen. "Through your bravery and aid during the flood you have won the trust and support of this queen and members of the army. I am prepared to make you a soldier in Her Majesty's army. What do you say to that?"

Think—and survive!

"I accept, your majesty."

"Way to go," said Bleato.

"Keep in mind that our soldiers stand together always," warned the queen. "You will share our shelter, our food, and our protection. In return you must become one of us, in times of peace and times of battle. And if the colony is destroyed, you shall be destroyed as well. Do you understand?"

Find protection—and live!

"Yes, your majesty."

She laid a foreleg on his shoulder. "Then from this moment onward, you are a Magyar soldier and a member of our colony—for good or for ill. Welcome."

6

"Hey, wait for me," squealed Bleato, as he scurried to keep up with Lawrence.

"Hop on!"

They were outside. The sky was deep blue and the clouds white and puffy. The piñon trees were fresh and green. The only remaining evidence of the storm was the swift-running water in the arroyo. Bleato and Lawrence climbed to the summit of Great Sun Stone and looked out.

"You can see the entire territory from up here," said Bleato. "This is Magyar country!"

"All this is yours?"

"Sure, let me show you," said Bleato. "Below is the colony, where you were a guest last night."

More than a guest, thought Lawrence, remembering their close call in the tunnel.

"Next to it is the Parade Ground," continued Bleato. "We have festivals and marches and stuff like that out there. We haven't used it too much lately. Not much to celebrate. But we have games and contests and races and wrestling, that kind of thing."

"You're probably the wrestling type," said Lawrence.

"Very funny," replied Bleato. "Now, look where I'm pointing. Start at the arroyo. It twists and turns right through the heart of our territory. See it go. The water's ripping right now. I sure wouldn't want to get caught in that. When it rains, the arroyo goes from a dry bed to a raging river in a moment. Little pools form afterwards and we store up on drinking water. Over there, that's Spider Bluff. Not a good place to hang out if you like living. Lots of very mean, cranky spider types that like to pop a few ants down before dinner."

"Kind of an appetizer?" asked Lawrence.

"Whatever. Now look next to Spider Bluff. There! The rock bowl. That's where we found you."

"Then I must have gone right through Spider Bluff," said Lawrence. "I was almost spider food on my first visit here."

"Yup, sounds about right," said Bleato. "Beyond that is Mount Baldy. We call it that because it's got nothing on top. You've got a nice head of hair, have I told you that?"

"You haven't."

"Well, consider it done. You can't see it from here, but next to Mount Baldy is Eagle Nest Pass. That's the end of our territory."

"Whose territory is beyond?"

"Creenio. Their colony is just over that pass."

"You don't go often, I'll bet," said Lawrence, with a smile.

"No trips planned in the near future," responded Bleato. "Now look over there. It's Cactus Butte. It's the hottest place in the territory. All rock and cactus. It's your basic scorched earth.

If you get caught out there during the day, you fry right up. Shriveled ant is not a nice thing. Ruins your whole day."

"I'll stay clear. What's over there?" Lawrence pointed behind Great Sun Stone.

"I don't know. That's outside our territory."

"You've never been there? But it's not far at all."

"It's outta the territory, pal. We don't go there. Against tradition."

"But don't you want to know what's there? It could be . . . anything."

"One thing you have to learn right off the bat is that we don't go outside the territory," Bleato said sternly.

Lawrence turned around. "What's over there, beyond Spider Bluff?"

"There's a whole bunch of colonies over there," said Bleato. "We make contact with them every now and then. They talk funny. A lot of them have been conquered by the Creenios, so they're not real happy in their work. The Creenios take most of the soldiers back to their colony as slaves."

"You have slaves?"

"The Creenios do. Some colonies have slaves, some don't. We don't. It's our big hearts, I guess. The Creenios, no such luck. Hearts made of rock. They run their colony on slaves. Thousands of them. They work them till they die in the fungus pits."

"What's that?"

Bleato said, "They grow the stuff inside the colony, in a huge pit. Lots of colonies do it, and the Creenios are the biggest. It's a foul-smelling, rotten place to be, from what I hear. You don't want to try to spend any quality time in the fungus pits."

"What do they do with the fungus?" asked Lawrence.

"They eat it. Pretty tasty actually. We once captured a group of Creenios carrying some."

"So the Creenios don't eat meat, just fungus?"

"No way, they're natural born killers," said Bleato. "They go on killing raids and slaughter anything in their path, like desert rats, snakes, scorpions, ants, anything that walks— they're history. Sephea and I were out on patrol one day, just a few of us, and we came across a Creenio killing party. We took cover and watched."

"They didn't see you?"

"Nope, they were too busy killing. But what a show."

"What did they do?"

"Oh, it was classic Creenio raiding party maneuvers," said Bleato. "They marched into this territory in one line, but then they split up into two and made a big circle. When the two lines reached each other, they turned and closed in toward the center. They came across a centipede and finished him off in seconds. They crawled all over cicadas, stink bugs, tarantulas—anything in their way—killing them and tearing them up. Not even flying things like moths were safe. They got on the wings and kept them from taking off. Then the army comes and—well, you get the rest. They tore them apart, chewed them up, and stored the food in their crops to take back to the colony. In no time the entire territory was stripped of all creatures. They never knew what hit them."

"What's that down there?" said Lawrence, seeing some movement in the valley.

"I don't see anything."

"Down there, near the Parade Grounds—it looks like the hillside is moving."

"Where?"

"There—coming out of the valley. . . ."

Bleato squinted. "It's . . . it's moving, isn't it?" he asked.

"Yeah, it looks like the desert is moving."

Bleato grew excited. "Come on, we gotta go," he shouted.

"Why?"

"The Creenios are invading—could be the whole army. We have to warn the others, if there's still time."

But, by the time they got down from Great Sun Stone, the Creenios had started the attack. Lawrence and Bleato found themselves caught between the two armies. Right in front of their eyes red soldiers cornered some black ants and pulled their abdomens from their bodies. Then Magyars rushed them and chased the Creenios back. But the reds retaliated.

Suddenly, a dozen red soldiers headed for Lawrence. Only as he was bounding away did he remember his sword. He yanked it out just in time. They were almost on top of him.

He remembered the queen's words. *"You are a Magyar now. If the colony is destroyed, you will be destroyed with it."*

Lawrence slowed down, luring them in by letting them think he was defenseless. Then he turned abruptly and plunged his sword. But the Creenios easily sidestepped his sword and fell on him. Their jaws closed around his legs.

"Looking bad, looking very bad," yelled Bleato.

But then a wave of Magyars raced over the hill and drove the red ants off before they could tear Lawrence apart.

"I'm finally in battle and I can't even fight," said Bleato, dejectedly.

"You be my eyes," shouted Lawrence, as more Creenios appeared.

"Okay, dive down," yelled Bleato. "Roll under them." Lawrence followed the directions and came up behind the red ants. Quickly, he jabbed his sword into the last one's gaster. The red ant let out a shriek.

"Now run!" yelled Bleato. Lawrence took off, with Bleato hanging onto his shoulder. "Take it from a runt. It is better to run and live than stay and die."

But the Creenios cut them off. Six headed toward them, snapping their mandibles and crunching their jaws. They reared up on their hind legs before attacking, and showed their puffy abdomens.

"Hey, you fellows need to lose a little weight," said Bleato. "Been slacking off on your workouts?"

The infuriated Creenios rushed in for the kill. Lawrence held them off with his sword long enough for the Magyars to drive them back. This can't go on much longer, thought Lawrence. I have this sword, but it barely bothers them. I can't fight them all.

A large Creenio came out of nowhere and wrapped his mandibles around his leg. Lawrence screamed as Bleato called for help. Another Creenio arrived and climbed onto Lawrence's back and positioned his stinger for the kill. Lawrence held his breath. But a moment later the red ant was hoisted into the air, and a Magyar twisted the life out of him. It was Homeron.

"Follow me," he said.

They raced over the hill and joined the fighting on the other side.

"Uh oh, not a good sign," said Bleato, looking about at the Magyar soldiers.

"Why?"

"These are the queen's guards," he replied. "They wouldn't be here unless they're the last ones left."

Homeron led the remaining Magyar soldiers toward the red ants.

"I guess I should go with them," said Lawrence, "but I can't fight very well, I'm afraid."

"Join the club," said Bleato.

But before they could join the others, the Magyars came running back over the rocks, chased by a hoard of Creenios. Just in time, Sephea gathered the few remaining soldiers and pushed them back. But not before many Magyars were badly hurt.

"Come quick," yelled a sentry. "It's Homeron. He's down."

They ran over the hill and found Homeron surrounded by several soldiers. They made way for Sephea and the rest of them. Homeron's lower half, from the abdomen down, had been ripped away and was now lying in the sand next to him. His front legs had been ripped out, too. One antenna was gone and the other badly damaged.

"Homeron," shouted Sephea. "What have they done to you?"

Homeron smiled weakly and motioned her forward. "You must listen carefully," he said. "There isn't much time. We have lost today. The Creenios will take the colony, but the Magyars must survive. Take these soldiers and go into the wilderness. One day you will return and win back the colony."

"I cannot leave the queen, Homeron," she replied. "You know that."

"Yes, you must," he replied, his voice beginning to fail. "Sephea, listen to me. We have been a colony for five thousand

generations. We may cease to be a colony today unless you do as I say. Go into the hills. Grow strong again. Then come back and free the queen. It is the only way."

"I . . . I just can't, Homeron," she said. But Homeron was no longer listening.

Sephea stared at his lifeless body for a few moments. Then she dropped to his side. "Homeron, don't go. You can't. Not now. I need you. I need you now more than ever." She paused, as if expecting him to respond. "I've never commanded before," she whispered. "I don't know if I can do it. We've never been outside the territory. Where will we go?"

"Well, you better figure it out quick!" squealed Bleato. "Cause look!"

Hundreds, thousands, then tens of thousands of red ants crowded the ridge above them, gathering their forces.

"It looks like the entire Creenio army," said Bleato in disbelief.

The soldiers parted and Antentius came forward. He stared at the few remaining Magyars and then threw back his head and laughed. And ten thousand ants laughed with him. The whole territory rang with their laughter.

Sephea stepped forward. "You are nothing but plague from the rat's den, Antentius," she yelled.

He smiled wickedly back at them. "I knew Magyar Hill would be mine," he replied. "I just didn't know it would be this soon. Your colony is finished. Surrender, and we will spare your pitiful lives."

"And live as slaves in your fungus pit?" said Sephea. "Never."

"Why not?" said Antentius. "You can keep your queen company."

Suddenly, the mass of Creenios opened and Queen Andulusia was pushed out onto the rocks. The soldiers poked her and prodded and snapped at her hind quarters with their mandibles. She tried not to show any distress, but it was clear that she was in pain. Queens do not ever come to the surface, so the light blinded her. Her captors brought her to the very edge of the ridge and pushed her toward the edge. The Magyars gasped, thinking she would soon plunge to certain death. But she hung onto a rock and dangled down.

Sephea's eyes were on fire. "How many soldiers do we have?" she demanded.

"About two thousand, maybe a few more," said a soldier.

"We shall attack," said Sephea. "Form up."

The soldiers took their positions.

Bleato ran up beside her. "Uh, hello," he said. "Hul-lo, Seph, what are we doing?"

"Not now, Bleato," said Sephea. "That is our queen and we will rescue her. I give the orders."

"If that's what you want, fine," he replied. "Fine. We'll charge up there and fifty thousand Creenios will tear us apart. It'll be a great battle. And Magyar Hill will die and the Creenios will control our valley for the next five thousand generations. If that's what you want, so be it."

"You'd leave the queen up there to die?" yelled Sephea, turning on Bleato. Her outburst shook the little ant, but he remained calm.

"They won't kill her," he responded. "They'll take her back to their colony. They've just got her there to lure you in. It's a trap."

"We will rescue our queen or die," insisted Sephea.

"Remember what Homeron said. Take to the hills or Magyar Hill is—history!"

Suddenly the wall of Creenios opened again and out came a boy.

"Tony!" yelled Lawrence.

"Hiya, Larry boy," he replied.

"What are you doing with—them?"

"Well, I'm not with a bunch of losers like you," responded Tony. "Things aren't looking too good for you, it seems."

"There are two of you?" said Sephea, dumbfounded.

"Yes, we came together."

"You're a spy," shouted the Magyar soldiers. "You're with him."

"No, no, I'm not, I promise," pleaded Lawrence.

"Then why is your friend helping the Creenios?"

"I don't know," responded Lawrence. "I don't know. But I'm not with him."

Antentius laughed. "Your foreigner is not one of us," he bellowed. "I already have my own foreigner."

"Give it up, Larry boy," said Tony. "You picked your army and I picked mine. You just lost, that's all. As usual, you're a loser. And Larry Boy, you might like to know that I have the turquoise stone."

Fear gripped Lawrence. "You have the stone?"

"Yup, we found it, and I'm on my way home. So long."

The queen still dangled from a rock. "Form up," ordered Sephea.

"Don't do it," whispered Bleato into her ear. "Head for the hills."

"Positions!" yelled Sephea.

"Remember Homeron's words, Seph, fight again another day. . . ."

"Att—"

A powerful shriek from the queen cut short her order to attack. Everyone stopped. She lost her grip on the rock and almost fell, but then got hold again. Gathering her strength, she said, "Go—now! Go—NOW!"

"Shut her up, you fools!" yelled Antentius. The soldiers instantly pulled the queen away from the rock and out of sight.

"Fall back," yelled Sephea. "Take to the hills."

"Follow them," yelled Antentius. "Catch them and kill them. No prisoners."

There was only one way out for the Magyars, and that was up a steep cliff. The Magyars quickly started up by four different routes, winding their way to the top. Many were not fast enough and the Creenios caught and killed them mercilessly. Others, seeing themselves cut off, turned on the advancing Creenios, sacrificing their lives to give the others more time to get away.

Lawrence and Bleato were near the back of the line, but the red ants could not catch up with them. They made their way up the cliff. At the top, a massive plateau opened up, flat ground filled with piñon trees and cholla cactus. A Magyar soldier shouted, "We're splitting up. Go your own way and meet up at Great Sun Stone after dark. Sephea's orders."

"The reds are right behind us," yelled Bleato. "How do you feel about running faster than those foreigner legs have ever run before?"

Lawrence dug his tattered sneakers into the desert sand. Away they sped down into a ravine, up a small arroyo and over the exposed roots of a juniper tree. Moments later, the reds appeared, almost on their heels.

"Get them," yelled the Creenios. "It's the foreigner."

Suddenly, they found themselves cut off by a giant ground cactus, a cholla with spindly arms and gnarled elbows, which spread out in a dozen direction on the ground, protecting itself with long, thin, razor-sharp needles. "In here," yelled Bleato, pointing at the cactus.

"Are you nuts?" asked Lawrence.

"It's okay, I've been inside these things before."

"I can't fit. I'll get sliced up."

"Think of it this way," said Bleato. "If you don't follow me, then say hi to them."

Looking up, he saw Creenio soldiers coming for them, with their mandibles open for attacking.

"Well, if you put it that way. . . ."

He dove into the cactus after Bleato, just ahead of the Creenios.

They found themselves in a forest of razors—that is, long cactus needles. At first Lawrence thought he would die if he moved one inch, but by standing up and holding the middle of the needles he found he could walk in. The red ants hovered outside the cactus but would not chance coming in. Gradually, as Lawrence and Bleato got deeper into the cactus, it grew shadowy. One slip and he'd be skewered, Lawrence knew, so he walked slowly, feeling his way. They came to a spider hole and eased away quietly. It was hard to know which way they were going, and they feared they might come out in front of the entire Creenio army.

"Hey, we're on a hill, right?" said Bleato.

"Yeah."

"So if we go uphill, we have to get away from them."

"Right."

They climbed slowly, making their way through the needles and finally came out on the very top, safely away from the Creenios. To avoid being spotted, they scurried into some rocks. They could easily see Magyar Colony and the Creenio soldiers down below. The red soldiers had gathered all the Magyar prisoners and Queen Andulusia on the Parade Grounds. The Creenios were taunting the helpless Magyars. The queen lay with her head down, while the red guards bit and snapped at her.

Bleato's eyes narrowed. "Look at how they treat our queen," he fumed. "They will pay for that." Standing on Lawrence's shoulder and peering down into the valley, he couldn't take his eyes off the horrifying scene.

"Let's go, we don't need to watch this," said Lawrence.

"Leave me alone," snapped Bleato. "I'm not leaving until I see what they do with the queen."

"Okay, okay," said Lawrence, stretching out on the rock. "We might as well get comfortable then." Down below the Creenios herded the Magyars and started them on a march.

"Where are they going?" asked Lawrence.

"Back to Creenio Colony," replied Bleato bitterly. "They are slaves now. The queen will continue to produce, but her offspring will be slaves as well."

They watched without speaking until the last Magyar prisoner disappeared out of sight.

"Let's go," said Bleato sharply, walking off.

They weren't going to make Great Sun Stone by sundown, but they started in that direction. After a while stumbling to keep up, Bleato gave in and hopped onto Lawrence's shoulder.

"You know what?" he said. It was the old Bleato speaking.

"What?"

"We've both lost our homes."

"That's true."

"That stone that Tony was talking about, the turquoise stone . . . what is it?"

"It's a long story, but basically it's my ride home."

"You mean you can't go home without it?" asked Bleato.

Lawrence nodded. "Tony's probably home by now and I'm stuck here forever."

"That's okay with me," said Bleato, smiling.

"Thanks, but I'd like to get home some time," he replied.

"Maybe you were meant to come here. Remember the prophecy."

"There's not really much I can do," said Lawrence.

"Let me tell you our history," said Bleato. "There's a legend about our first queen."

"What is it?"

"Five thousand generations ago, Queen Riadda had to leave her homeland due to drought. Her guards accompanied her on her journey. The Craneans, ancestors to the Creenios, set upon her and tried to kill her. All the queen's guards were killed."

"What happened to the queen?"

"That's where the story gets good," continued Bleato. "They threw her off Rockface Cliff, and no one falls from there and lives. But legend has it the winds carried her to safety."

"She wasn't hurt?" asked Lawrence in disbelief.

"She floated down. She was found by a stranger, a foreigner from a far off land. Sort of like you. He kept her alive for a long time. Together they wandered the desert until they founded Magyar Hill. There she had her first offspring. Before the foreigner disappeared, he told our queen that in the future when the colony is threatened, another will come to save them."

Lawrence blinked.

"But no one was there today to save the queen," said Bleato, his voice faltering. "If I were bigger, I could have fought the Creenios, I could have protected the queen, I could have—"

"I couldn't do much either, I'm afraid, so I don't think much of your prophecy."

"Come on," said Bleato, "we better find a place to sleep the night. We'll make it to Great Sun Stone in the morning."

At the end of a cactus, they settled into a hollowed-out fruit. It would protect them for the night. Soon Lawrence drifted off to sleep.

"Go over the mountain," said a voice. "Lead them over this mountain." Lawrence turned and looked up. "It will be dangerous. There is nowhere to hide. The birds may come for you, but keep going." "They will not follow me," said Lawrence. "I am a foreigner." "If you want to live, it is the only way," said the voice. "There will be a pool of water and a mountain. Follow the path over the mountain and you will discover a beautiful valley. Lead them there. Do not stop there, but keep going. You will then see a rock wall with small black holes. Follow along. This is the way you must go, if you care to live. Otherwise you will die here." "I am afraid," said Lawrence. "The old Lawrence would be afraid, but the old Lawrence is dead—"

Lawrence awoke abruptly. It was morning and the desert was just coming alive. He roused Bleato hurriedly.

"What? What?" he said, rubbing his eyes open. "Can't an ant get his beauty sleep around here?"

"We have to find Sephea."

"What for?" asked Bleato.

"Because—something has happened."

7

"They aren't gonna like it," warned Bleato. "I'm telling you."

"It's our only chance," pleaded Lawrence.

"How do you know?" asked Sephea. "How can you be so sure?"

"I can't be sure," he replied, bowing his head. "But I think so."

Bleato piped up. "They've never been outside the territory before. And under that tough soldier exterior, we've got a bunch of whiners on our hands," he said.

Sephea was deep in thought. It meant going outside the territory, and all because of a dream—a foreigner's dream! But it was a chance. The night crawlers had killed hundreds of them during the night, and they needed shelter.

"I don't know if they'll go," said Sephea, her voice hesitating. "They won't leave the territory," she said. "They've been told all their lives never to leave the territory."

"You'll order them to go," said Bleato. "I know this command stuff is new to you, but you'll get the hang of it."

"I'm . . . I'm so afraid I'll do the wrong thing."

"What choice do we have?" said Bleato. "I ain't staying here another night to get eaten by some tarantula, thank you very much," he replied.

"All right, we'll go," said Sephea, "but I sure hope there's something to your dream, Lawrence."

"So do I," he said under his breath. "So do I."

Sephea quickly gathered the soldiers and they moved out almost immediately, up the arroyo. An hour later they passed Great Sun Stone, which marked the end of their territory. The soldiers started to get jittery.

"Here come the whiners, just like I told you," said Bleato.

They soon passed out of the Magyar territory. Now they were marching in completely unknown territory. Gradually, there was a far-away humming sound. But Lawrence could not identify it. The soldiers halted.

"Here we go," said Bleato. "They're gonna be trouble. What a bunch of babies! Just because we haven't been out of the territory in five thousand generations, that doesn't mean it's new or anything."

"We will go no further," said the soldiers. "It is against the laws of the Magyars. The law forbids it."

"The queen, I might remind you gaster-heads, is in a Creenio fungus pit right now waiting for us to come rescue her," said Bleato.

"Why are we following the foreigner anyway?" yelled the soldiers. "Let's kill him and be done with him."

"Don't be even stupider than you already are," said Bleato.

"I've got it!" yelled Lawrence suddenly. "That sound. I know what it is. Listen! Do you hear it?" They all strained to hear. "I know what it is. It's water. Water!"

"I hear it," yelled Bleato. "I think."

"I hear—something," said Sephea. "It sounds like. . . ."

"It's up ahead," yelled Lawrence. "Let's go see."

There was a long pause while the ants thought it over.

Bleato addressed the guards. "If you kill him now and then find water just up ahead, you're going to feel pretty stupid, aren't you?" said Bleato.

Lawrence led the way. "Come on, come on." The ants slowly followed him. He turned a corner and the sound got louder. And louder. And then there it was, a perfectly round pool of water, just like the one from his dream, at the base of a mountain. The ants ran to drink from the pool.

Lawrence walked over. Spray from a waterfall floated over him, cooling his face and arms.

"What do we do now?" Sephea asked, coming up beside him.

He pointed to the mountain, the one from his dream. "We go over," he said.

Sephea sent out her best soldiers to scout a path to the top. They quickly laid down scent and the army followed single file. It was slow going, though. At one point a flicker circled overhead and the ants took cover. But it went off in search of an easier meal. They continued on.

"If we're caught up here at night, we'll all be dead by morning," said Sephea.

The sun was just beginning to set when Lawrence, in the lead, scrambled to the top. I hope it's there, he said to himself. What if it's not? What if I have led the last of the Magyars to a mountaintop to be killed by night crawlers? All because of a dream! He threw himself over the top, and there it was below—the valley from his dream. Sephea reached the top next.

"Is this it?" she asked, her voice quivering with excitement.

"That's it," he said, confidently.

The ants quickly poured into the valley. There clear mellow pools of water, seeds and sweet cactus fruit were waiting for them. The valley was full of yellow and purple cactus flowers. A light breeze cooled them. The hunters then went off in search of insects and came back with a feast. Gradually, it grew dark.

"We must find a safe place for the night," said Sephea. She looked at Lawrence.

"That way," he said, pointing to a ravine. He led them over a ridge and down into a smooth rock bowl. Giant cliffs towered on all sides. Set into the cliffs were small black holes, just as he had been told in his dream. Sephea ordered scouts up to investigate. They hurried to the black holes, probed with their antennas, and disappeared. Reappearing a moment later, they shouted, "Caves! Caves!"

Sephea turned to Lawrence. "We're safe," she said. "You've done it."

The Magyar army—what was left of it—scrambled up the cliff face and scurried into the cave openings. Inside it was dusty and cramped and dark. Slowly, chanting as they walked, they made their way deeper into the cave.

Suddenly, they were surrounded and cut off by a vast army of black ants.

"I am the leader of the Pandamarians," boomed a voice. "We wish you no harm."

"Pantara?" said Sephea, stepping forward.

"Sephea? Is that you?"

"Pantara!" Sephea stepped forward and the two touched antennas and reared up on hind legs.

"Well, whaddaya know?" said Pantara. "It's the Magyars! Send out the hunter-gatherers and let's have a feast."

In no time the hunters returned with grasshoppers, stink bugs, beetles, crickets, yellow jackets, moths and more. The gatherers brought back seeds and cactus fruit. The food was quickly separated into piles and laid out in the cave. The leaders then sat down in a semi-circle in front of the mingling armies. Pantara rose and looked sternly at the soldiers. The room grew silent.

"Assembled soldiers, warriors, great ones, let's do what we do best—eat!" yelled Pantara. And they dug in. Everyone, that is, but Lawrence, who just stared at the dead bugs and couldn't bring himself to eat them despite his hunger.

"Come on, you gotta eat something," Bleato managed between mouthfuls.

Lawrence tried to eat the seeds, but they were hard and stuck to his back teeth.

"How about this?" said Bleato, passing a dead bug. "It's grasshopper."

Lawrence took a piece of the greasy midsection and held it in his fingers.

"Just eat it," said Bleato. "Don't think about it."

Lawrence closed his eyes and took a bite. The taste of the grasshopper, still warm from the afternoon sun, tasted . . . well . . . all right. He chewed faster.

"Hey, that's good," said Lawrence. "I'll have some more."

"Someone I see is starting to eat like a Magyar," said Sephea, passing by at that moment. Moonlight filled the chamber. Lawrence smiled, as he dove into the food. He stuffed himself with cicada, moth, stink bug, centipede, and many desert creatures he could not even identify. It dawned on him that he had not eaten for several days, except for a little water and some seeds and a little cactus fruit. But not a real meal, not a meal like he had . . . at home. He stopped himself, because he had promised himself that he would not think about home and his mother and father and room or—anything. But now the memories flooded in.

The simple things came back to him—getting into his mom's minivan, seeing his dad come home from the newspaper office. They were having dinner together, and his mom was laughing at something he'd said. The smell of his mother's chicken and mashed potatoes rose up and filled his brain. He could almost taste the food. Suddenly, he was in his room with his soccer trophies. Music was playing from his portable CD. His mother came in and smiled at him.

"Time for bed," she said.

"I'm sorry, Mom," he said. "I'm sorry I ran away."

"We miss you," she said. "How are things where you are?"

"Okay," he said. "But I want to be home again," he replied. "I want to be home where it's safe and warm and I can just be myself again."

"You're growing up, Lawrence. Are you coming home soon?" she asked.

"I don't know. I'm trying."

"When you're ready," she replied. And she was gone, the door closing behind her.

The door flew open again, but it was not his mother this time but Dennis Yazzie, the Navajo from the cabin. Dennis knelt in front of him.

"Don't forget the stone," he said. "It will bring you home. Find the stone."

"Tony has it, and he's gone home with it," replied Lawrence. "I'm here forever. Why did you do this to me, Dennis? Why?"

"You needed to do this, to go on this journey," said the Navajo. "You need to learn not to be afraid."

"Now I'm really afraid."

"Believe in yourself," said Dennis. "Believe that you can make it. You cannot go home until you believe in yourself."

"Hey, you gonna eat that stink bug?" A voice brought him out of his daydream. "Hey, what's the matter with you? What's wrong with your eyes? There's water coming out of them," said Bleato.

Using the sleeve of his tattered shirt, Lawrence wiped his eyes. He looked around. The ants were finishing up and the games had begun. There was wrestling, antenna boxing, and "hop racing," where the ants reared up on their hind legs and hopped across the chamber.

The Magyars and the Pandamarians mingled freely, sometimes joining together in teams. The competition ended with the fiercest Magyar, a soldier named Turroses, and the mightiest Pandamarian, Lussus, facing off in a battle of strength in the center of the chamber. Both sides cheered for their soldier and there were many throw-downs and jaw marks before it was over. Everyone cheered when a draw was finally called and the two mighty warriors touched antennas in respect.

"Now I want you all to see something," said Pantara. "Come with me."

As many as could fit followed him into a chamber deep in the cave. The leaders crowded around the far wall. Lawrence ducked down and scrambled between the ants to reach the front. "Now take a look at this," said Pantara. Something was embedded in the wall, a tiny speck of something, something black but deep in the clear amber rock.

"Ah," said Bleato, in a sudden cry. Then the others saw it and cried out.

"What? What is it?" asked Lawrence.

"It's an ant," said Pantara.

"An ant?"

"An amber ant. Sometimes an ant gets stuck and dies in a sticky spot and then gets covered over by a clear rock. We call it amber rock because it's yellow and see-through."

"An ant?" asked Lawrence. "In the rock?"

"Not just any ant," said Sephea, solemnly. "It's an ancient Magyar."

"How can you tell?" the soldiers yelled.

"It has the markings," replied Sephea. "It's got our head, Magyar eyes, and the shape of our bodies. It is very old, many thousands of generations, I'd say."

A hush fell over the Magyars. "Then this must be . . ." said Bleato.

"Yes, this was the home of Queen Riadda," said Sephea. "These are the Caves of Anraxia, which we all learned about in the nursery. When Queen Riadda set out, it was from here. So we did not leave our territory for the wilderness after all."

"Well, whaddaya know about that?" said Pantara. "And I thought it was just another dead ant."

Later, the leaders assembled in the main chamber. Lawrence was allowed to sit just outside the circle and listen. Bleato, for once, was quiet and subdued, respectful of the leaders. Word had gone out to the other colonies and their leaders had come to meet the mighty Magyars and hear their story. Sephea led off. She told about the civil war between their two queens, Andulusia and Meetrio, and how it had weakened the colony. When she told how the Creenios had started to push into their territory, the leaders all murmured in agreement, nodding their huge heads. Sephea then told how the flood came and how they had lost many of their soldiers. Then she recounted the battle for Magyar Hill, and how Homeron had died on the battlefield, and how they had fled into the wilderness.

"This very morning," she finished, "we set out and traveled up the Great Arroyo until we reached the falls, and then came over the mountains and into the Valley of Anraxia and finally here. Now you have heard our story."

Pantara whistled. "Well, I never," he said. "The mighty Magyars pushed out of their colony. Impossible!"

"Now, Pantara, tell us how a band of Pandamarians could end up here."

"Ah, that's easy." The others leaned forward, cocking their heads, all eyes on him. Pantara seemed the perfect showman to Lawrence, timing his speech perfectly, taking center stage, holding his audience still and attentive.

"The Creenios—they came to conquer us, just like every other colony in this room," he said. The leaders nodded sadly. "We went out to the battlefield and met them, just like our ancestors did time and again."

The leaders knew this story well, for they too had been defeated by the Creenios in battle.

"But the Creenios routed us. But the queen was still safe inside the colony. The Creenios offered us a deal. If we surrendered and agreed to provide slaves, they would let us keep our queen. But those Creenios, they're lying every time they take a breath, so I refused to go along. My own leaders exiled me and these others here with you tonight. And was I right? You betcha. Right after the surrender, the Creenios marched right in and took our queen back to their colony. Now she produces slaves for them and we live without a queen. Soon our colony will die out."

"How did you come here?"

"We walked twenty moons in the open before finding this place," said Pantara. "It was a cave, and we needed shelter."

The leaders all nodded. The story was familiar to them.

"The same thing happened to all of you?" asked Sephea.

One of the leaders rose in response. "I am Maroi, leader of the Nadarians," she said. "We were once strong and thriving, a brave colony of a hundred thousand soldiers. Then the Creenios conquered us and now we live under the control of those red devils. Our queen is captive in their colony, our soldiers have been reduced to ten thousand, and our colony is dying."

Sephea looked around the circle. "And the rest of you?" she asked.

All told the same story.

Sephea bowed her head in thought. It was obvious who the leader was now—Sephea. And not just because she was a Magyar. She was just naturally in command. There was silence in the chamber for several seconds. All eyes settled on Sephea. Then she looked up quickly.

"Then we shall join together and defeat the Creenios," she declared. There was a stunned silence. "We shall march against them and bring out our queens," said Sephea.

Pantara asked, "And just how are you gonna do that, Seph? You've got a few thousand soldiers and we've got a few thousand, and that ain't gonna do it. The Creenios have hundreds of thousands of the fiercest soldiers who would like nothing better than to have us for breakfast."

Sephea's eyes flashed. "That's why the first thing we have to do is get our soldiers back," she said. "Who's with me?"

8

The next morning, a guard woke Lawrence from a deep sleep before sunup. After the council had ended, sleep had come quickly and now he struggled to wake up. The guard moved down the line waking up all the Magyars. Guards from other colonies were waking their soldiers as well.

"You'd think they'd let a guy sleep a little, wouldn't you?" grumbled Bleato. "I mean, this wandering around the wilderness makes a guy tired."

"Come on, let's go see what's up," said Lawrence.

Normally, early morning was time for hunting, to find and bring in the night crawlers who dallied a bit too long in the open. But this morning, if it could be called morning because the moon was still up and only a hint of dawn could be seen over the mountains, the soldiers had no thoughts of food.

"What's going on?" asked Bleato.

On the smooth gray rock the leaders were meeting. The soldiers were forming up in long columns. After the conference, the leaders gave the signal and started marching their soldiers out of the bowl. They headed for the mountains.

"I don't think I can march," said Bleato, looking pale. "I don't feel too good. Can I ride for a while?"

"Sure." He hopped up and found a soft spot. It wasn't his usual position. Normally he stood on the shoulder and gripped hard. But now he crawled into the tattered collar.

"I'm going to sleep."

"Get some rest," replied Lawrence. "I'll wake you when we've defeated the Creenios." Bleato smiled weakly and put his head down.

"You'll be okay," said Lawrence. "I'll take care of you."

The little ant didn't reply, and soon Lawrence forgot about him and concentrated on the march. It was the fastest march yet. Sephea led the Magyars out of Anraxia Valley, over the mountain, past the pool, and down into the arroyo. As they reached Cactus Butte, the sun was just coming up over the peaks. And as it did, Lawrence felt the temperature rise in an instant.

"No stopping under any circumstances," ordered Sephea. "We have to get across Cactus Butte quickly before the heat of the day, or we will die on the rocks."

They set off at a forced march. Lawrence had to trot to keep up. Without sunblock, he had grown red and brown and red and brown again in his days here. Now the sun beat down, turning his skin to a crisp.

"Gonna be a hot day," he said.

Bleato groaned, but said nothing.

"You're gonna be okay, little buddy," said Lawrence.

The Magyar soldiers were beginning to feel the heat, he knew, by the way they grew silent and determined. They simply marched ahead, never varying their speed, across the scorching rocks. The heat rose in waves. It got through his shoes and his feet began to burn. Twice they passed shady places, but Sephea would not even think about stopping. Lawrence grew wobbly and sick to his stomach, but kept on. The sun was roasting them. They walked for hours, until Lawrence lost track of time and place and thought only of reaching the other side. Finally, the rocks marking the end of Cactus Butte came into sight.

"There's shade and water in those rocks," yelled a soldier.

Lawrence was stumbling. "Bleato, we made it, little buddy, we're there, and there's water!" he said. He got no reply. "Bleato?" Lawrence gently felt for him in the folds of his shirt. Nothing. He ripped off his shirt. "Bleato? Bleato? Where are you?" There was no sign of him. "He must have fallen off back there somewhere," Lawrence yelled.

The soldiers shrugged. "He's just a runt," said one.

"He wasn't just a runt," screamed Lawrence, as his eyes scanned the endless rock of Cactus Butte, and saw the heat rising.

"Come on, Lawrence," said Sephea. "I'm sorry to lose him, but we've got to get out of this heat or we'll die."

Lawrence glanced at her, then back at the rocks. The sun was high. The rocks seemed to be moving in the waves of rising heat. He had had nothing to drink all day. His legs were shaking, his throat parched. But slowly at first, then running, back he went onto Cactus Butte.

"There's nothing we can do, Lawrence," yelled Sephea. "No sense in both of you dying."

"He's probably dead already," said a guard.

"He was my responsibility," Lawrence yelled back. "I have to find him."

"Come back, Lawrence," Sephea pleaded. "We have to think of the colony."

"Don't worry, I'll be back," he called.

Lawrence kept going into the bleak, hot desert. A short time later he looked back, but couldn't see the soldiers. Around him was an endless expanse of rock. The sun was at its peak now. It's the heat of the day, he thought. Bad time to be out here. He walked for another hour. Then he stopped. He was having trouble walking and his throat was closing up. Looking around, the rocks grew blurry.

He thought in panic, what if Bleato crawled off to the side? What if he got carried off by a bird or spider? I'll walk and walk and walk and never find him. And then what? And then . . . I have to turn back. But what if Bleato is alive and just ahead, waiting for me to come back? I can't let him down. When I first got here, it was Bleato who stuck up for me. He was my friend. I can't leave him here.

Lawrence couldn't help himself and sat down. Everything seemed hazy, so he wasn't sure if he was seeing things when a black bird landed nearby. It was jet black with an ivory colored beak, long and hooked. Am I dreaming? Am I seeing things? Am I dying? he thought. He rubbed his eyes, and sure enough a giant crow was hopping towards him. His face was sleek and hard, his barrel chest shiny and smooth, his eyes small but clear. Strangely, Lawrence was not afraid, and just smiled as it approached.

"Haaaa-looooo," said the bird.

"Hello," Lawrence replied. "Are you here for me?"

"I have been sent by Dennis," said the bird. "I'm here to tell you not to give up."

"It's so hot," replied Lawrence. "I just want to go to sleep."

"No, no, no, don't do that, whatever you do! You'll be crispy dead in no time."

"You're a nice bird, a very nice bird," said Lawrence, "but I'm just . . . very . . . tired. . . ."

"Hey, hey, hey, don't make this harder than it has to be," said the bird.

And with that the crow took Lawrence in his beak and gently placed him on his back. Somehow in his woozy state Lawrence knew to grab the bird's neck in his hands like it was a horse. The bird's wings flapped and with one tremendous motion they were airborne. The cool air revived Lawrence and he soon regained his strength. When he looked down, he was so frightened by the height that he lost his grip and almost plunged off the side. But he pulled himself back up.

"There!" said the crow, suddenly.

"What?"

"Your friend, the one you're looking for."

"Bleato?"

"We have to hurry, there's a spider going for him right now. Hold on."

The crow plunged into a dive. The wind screamed past Lawrence's face and the ground rushed at them at an alarming speed. They made a hard landing between the spider and Bleato, who was motionless on the rock.

"Beat it," said the crow to the spider.

"Aw, come on," said the spider, backing off. "I ain't eaten in three days. Give a spider a break."

"I'm telling you, push off!"

"You crows have such a high opinion of yourselves, don't you?" said the spider, as he scurried off.

"Bleato!" Lawrence said, picking him up.

"You came back," whispered Bleato.

"Look, little buddy, we've got a ride back."

On the other side of the mesa, Sephea and her soldiers had decided to wait in the shade of some rocks overlooking Great Sandy Plain, but it was getting late.

"We can't wait much longer," said a soldier.

"We have to meet up with the the other colonies," argued another, in disgust. "We can't ruin the whole plan because of the foreigner and a runt. We have to move now."

Sephea wheeled on them, her eyes flashing. "Let me tell you something. That foreigner you're talking about saved the queen during the flood. Maybe you'd like to tell the queen when we rescue her that you left him on Cactus Butte?" The soldiers looked down and said nothing. "I didn't think so," Sephea went on. "And that runt? Well, maybe he can't fight, but he's smarter than all of you put together. We wait until I say it's time to leave."

Leaving the soldiers to their grumbling, Sephea walked out onto the rock. The soldiers stayed in the shade. She knew they were right, that she should have left them long ago, but she couldn't bring herself to do it. Just a little while longer, she said to herself.

"Look, look! What's that?" said a sentry.

Through the waves of heat rising off the rocks, a small black speck appeared. It was coming toward them, growing in size.

"Someone is running toward us," yelled the sentry.

"It can't be Lawrence," said a soldier. "He couldn't run that fast in this heat—not after all this time out there."

"Impossible," said the others. "It must be a Creenio, and we'll be found out." The ants scurried to hide.

"No," said Sephea, recognizing him in the distance, "it's Lawrence."

He came into view, with Bleato on his shoulder looking chipper and happy. The astounded soldiers raced out to welcome them.

"You probably thought I was a goner?" said Bleato. "Well, come on, this is Bleato we're talking about here."

"We have to move quickly, we're late because of you two," said Sephea, trying to be stern with them but clearly relieved. Lawrence and Bleato joined the rest, as they moved out. As they came over a rocky ridge, the entire Great Sandy Plain suddenly opened up before them. It was a startling sight. As far as Lawrence could see, there was nothing but a vast expanse of sand with an occasional clump of desert grass. At the far end of this giant rectangle of sand was a hill of rocks. It looked climbable.

At the other end was a giant anthill—Creenio Colony. It was so much bigger than Magyar Hill. Lawrence could not believe that an anthill could be so big.

And coming and going from this massive earthworks— red ants! Creenios! Thousands upon thousands of them, tens of thousands, perhaps a hundred thousand—just below them. Soldiers were standing guard, hunters were returning and forcing insects down the tunnels, and builders were carrying sand from inside the colony and piling it nearby. Clearly, they were seeing a mighty civilization.

We're going to fight them? thought Lawrence in horror. We're going to take on all of Creenio Colony—and beat them? No way. What is Sephea thinking? We can't get the queen out. We're just going to get ourselves killed.

Sephea quietly ordered the ants to gather around, and Lawrence obeyed, but reluctantly. She then led them behind some rocks to the other side of the great ring of sand. They entered a small clearing. They spotted a Creenio scout on his rounds, so they crossed the clearing and found refuge in some chamisa.

"Look behind you," said Bleato quietly. Lawrence turned around and was so frightened from the sight that he fell backwards. They were standing only inches from the edge of a magnificent cliff. The bottom was so far away that he could barely make out the landscape below.

"Where are we?" asked Lawrence, staring out.

"It's Rockface Cliff."

"This is the place. . . ."

"Yes, where Queen Riadda was thrown off and floated to safety."

"Impossible," exclaimed Lawrence. "No one could live after going off here."

"Quiet!" yelled the guard.

Bleato shrugged at the guard. "You're not worried about a couple hundred thousand Creenios, are you?" he said, rolling his eyes. "Soldiers today!"

They waited. And waited. Finally, the sun began to set and it cooled off a bit. With nothing to drink all day, his throat was parched, but Lawrence found that like the ants his own personal pains didn't matter much anymore.

Suddenly, up ahead, a few hundred black ants appeared in the clearing.

"There are the Magyar slaves!" said Sephea. "Be ready."

"What are we doing?" whispered Lawrence.

"We're going to try to recapture them," replied Bleato.

"I get it now," said Lawrence, drawing his sword.

Red guards were prodding the slaves forward, forcing them to find vegetation and chew it to bring back to the colony for the fungus.

When they had reached the narrowest part of the small valley, Sephea gave the signal and the Magyars poured out into the clearing from all directions. They fell upon the Creenio guards, who were taken by surprise by an attack this close to their colony. The guards fell back and the attackers over-whelmed them. The Magyar slaves immediately turned on their guards and before Lawrence could swing his sword once the battle was over. But a few guards escaped and ran back to-ward the colony.

"Time to beat it," said Bleato.

Sephea ordered a retreat over Eagle Nest Pass. Now they were a few thousand strong. But the alarm sounded and the Creenio soldiers came flooding out of the colony. Antentius could be seen giving orders to his soldiers. The Creenios started off at a run for the pass, to cut off Sephea. Pantara took a few hun-dred soldiers back and met them head on, blocking the way to the pass, to give Sephea time to get over. When it looked like the Creenios would break through, Pantara ordered a retreat and headed for the pass.

When the order to fall back was given, Lawrence took one last swipe with his sword, then turned and ran. He headed up the path until he was fifty paces from the top of the pass.

The last of the Magyar slaves were just going over. Lawrence was about to slip over the pass to safety, when he saw the first wave of red ants coming up the hill. He turned to hold them back until the rest of the Magyars made it over. As he did, his foot slipped and he tumbled off a ledge and rolled down into a ravine.

"Get up, get up," yelled Bleato, who had survived the fall by ducking under his arm.

"I can't," said Lawrence. "My leg. I can't move it."

"I'll get help," said Bleato, as he scrambled up the hillside and disappeared over the top.

In the next instant the hillside was overrun by red ants. Hundreds of them occupied the pass. Antentius rushed to the top. There he stopped and looked. The Magyars were gone, blending into the desert on the other side of the pass.

"Let them go," grumbled Antentius. "They have no colony. They will die out there anyway."

"Antentius! Look there!"

He turned and spotted Lawrence in the ravine. Several soldiers crowded around him, poking and biting him.

"Hey, cut that out," yelled Lawrence.

The soldiers wanted to kill him, but Antentius called them off. He ambled down the slope and stood there towering over Lawrence.

"Let's see how the foreigner likes Creenio hospitality," he said. "Throw him in the fungus pit." His soldiers went to grab him.

"Keep your legs off me," shouted Lawrence. "I can walk on my own." He limped slowly back toward the colony, surrounded by a pack of red ants. Suddenly, he felt light tapping on the inside of his leg. He carefully took a look downward, pretending to be checking his wound. There, hiding on his pant leg, was Bleato.

"How did you get back?" whispered Lawrence.

"You didn't leave me on Cactus Butte, did you?" replied Bleato.

"Oh, brother," sighed Lawrence. "Now we're both in for it."

9

Down the guards went into the dark, damp, humid colony, dragging Lawrence and Bleato, biting and stinging them. Lawrence tried to protect himself with his sword, but the Creenios disarmed him and after that he had no weapon. He smelled something rich and thick, like a heavy oil, and as they got deeper down into the colony and the smell got stronger, Lawrence struggled to get air.

"Bleato!" he whispered, "I can't breathe, I can't breathe."

He was fighting for every breath. I can't do this for long, he said to himself. A little tickle developed in his throat. Then he started to cough. It became a stronger cough, and stronger still, until he thought his chest would rip apart. The guards just laughed.

"Hang on, Lawrence," whispered a voice.

Finally, when he had almost passed out from the pain, they stopped. The guards picked him up and tossed him in a pit.

"So you want to be a Magyar?" said a guard. "Then we're going to treat you like one." They went off laughing.

"Where are we?" Lawrence managed, between coughing spasms.

"We're in the fungus pit," replied Bleato.

"Bleato, can't breathe, can't breathe . . ." he said.

"I'll be right back. Don't go anywhere till I get back."

Lawrence lay on his side, wheezing, not able to respond.

After what seemed like hours, Bleato reappeared out of the darkness. "Here, put this over your mouth," he said. "Now take a breath." Lawrence started slowly. It was like breathing through a wet towel.

"It's okay," he managed. "I can breathe a little. What is it?"

"A petal from a cactus flower," said Bleato. "The slaves brought them in for the fungus and they smuggled it to me. Come on, crawl up the side and let me show you where we are."

Every muscle in his body hurt. His shoulder burned from the fall into the pit. His arms were raw from being dragged. He was still dizzy and sick to his stomach, but Lawrence managed to drag himself to the top of the pit.

Just like inside Magyar Hill, he could see easily in the eerie green light glowing from the walls. He noticed two gigantic, fuzzy, weird-looking balls in the middle of the chamber, surrounded by hundreds of working slaves.

"What's that?" whispered Lawrence, pointing.

"It's the fungus," said Bleato.

"It's huge. You eat that stuff?"

"Fungus is a real delicacy in these parts," said Bleato. "I like mine with juniper berries."

"I'll order you some," said Lawrence.

"Look over there. See, the slaves are carrying bits of vegetation—piñon, sage, grass, whatever. The guards make them haul as much as they can handle. Now look at that pile over there. They place the vegetation in that pile and go back up for more."

"Then what happens to the vegetation?"

"Oh, then the chewing starts. See those slaves over there. They're all chewing, chewing, chewing the vegetation into a mush."

"Then what?"

"They plant it," replied Bleato. "Look over there. See that bunch of little balls? They start them there and then move them to the center when they get big."

"It smells so horrible."

"Not to us," said Bleato. "Ants think it tastes pretty good. In fact, this particular fungus is why the Creenios are so strong. They grow their own food. Everybody eats more. They have more babies. Babies make soldiers. And whamo—we're slaves."

"Those slaves over there," said Lawrence, "they're Magyars. I thought we rescued all of them."

"Not all," replied Bleato sadly. "There's slaves here from all the colonies—Pandamarians, Burgans, Toledians, Fremmians, Marses, you name it, they're here, availing themselves of Creenio hospitality. When the Creenios take over a colony, they bring half the soldiers back here as slaves. That way the fungus gets tended while making the colony weak and defenseless."

Lawrence started to cough again. "Hold the petal to your mouth," warned Bleato. "I'll sneak out and get more petals later if you need them."

Soon Lawrence adapted to the stale air and even managed to grab some sleep. Bleato sneaked out for some cactus fruit and the juice revived him. Suddenly, the guard appeared around the edge of the pit.

"Come with us, foreigner," said a guard.

"Where am I going?" replied Lawrence, as he scrambled out of the pit with Bleato hiding in his collar.

"The queen has summoned you," he replied.

Something was different. The guards were polite to him and there was no pinching or biting or stinging. On the way, they passed many chambers—seed rooms, nurseries, eating halls. They moved steadily upward.

"In here," ordered the guard finally. They emerged into a large chamber crowded with red ants. Every antenna was at attention and they all turned to stare. The crowd parted slowly as he walked and then closed behind him.

"We're in the queen's chamber," whispered Bleato, climbing up behind his ear to talk to him easily. "You can tell because these ants just stand around doing nothing. It's the same everywhere."

Suddenly, Lawrence spotted Antentius and his legs almost buckled. But Antentius was smiling and beckoned him to approach.

"Watch out for that character," said Bleato.

Tony was there too, standing in the back.

"I would like to introduce you to Queen Natoria," said Antentius, politely. Lawrence looked at the queen. She was surrounded by an army of attendants licking and rubbing her.

Lawrence didn't like the look on her face. It was cold and haughty. There was a hint of nobility about it, but unlike Queen Andulusia, she seemed hard and unfriendly.

"Are you enjoying your stay with us?" she asked, trying to seem interested.

"Oh, yeah, it's really been great," whispered Bleato.

Ignoring him, Lawrence replied, "I am a slave, your majesty."

"Really?" asked the queen, pretending to be astonished. "What a terrible, horrible mistake we've made. Someone apologize for me."

A dozen courtiers rushed forward and apologized. Lawrence could hear Bleato laughing.

The queen continued. "Your friend Tony here has explained everything, and we see that you didn't belong in the fungus pit at all," said the queen. "So you don't have to go back."

"Watch it, something's going on," whispered Bleato.

"Did you say something?" said the queen. "Speak up."

"Explain what?" replied Lawrence, shifting uneasily. "What did Tony explain?"

"Oh, we thought you were a Magyar soldier," said Antentius. "But Tony explained to us that you weren't."

"But I am!" said Lawrence.

"Hey, we're trying to get out of here," whispered Bleato. "You don't have to tell them everything."

"But you're from another territory," said Antentius.

"It's true, I'm not from here," replied Lawrence.

"And because you come from somewhere else," Antentius interrupted, "you owe them nothing!"

"Well, I. . . ."

"In fact," said the queen, "we feel so badly about being such terrible hosts that we're prepared to send you home immediately."

"Home?" Lawrence yelled loudly, then caught himself. "You mean I can go home?"

"Yes," said the queen, with a sly smile. Tony nodded furiously in the back. "Your friend Tony here has the turquoise stone and you two can go home at any time."

Lawrence stared at Antentius. "But what about the Magyars?" he asked.

"Well, Lawrence, you must understand," he replied patiently. "These are our ways here in the desert. We fight. We die. You must not stand in the way of that. And you cannot change the course of our history, no matter what."

"It's okay," whispered Bleato. "Go home. We'll be okay."

"But there is one thing we'd like you to tell us before we let you go," said the queen, in a silky voice. "I think that's only fair."

"Here it comes," said Bleato.

"What is it?" said Lawrence.

"You've come from the hiding place of Sephea and the Magyars," said Antentius. "We'd like you to tell us where it is—and then you can go home."

"But you'll . . . ." stammered Lawrence.

"That's right, we'll go there and kill them," said Antentius. "But it is no business of yours. You are not one of them."

"Larry Boy," Tony said, rushing over, "tell them and let's get out of here."

"I . . . I can't do that."

"If you don't," snapped the queen, showing her true feelings, "then you can rot in the fungus pit for the rest of your life."

"But they're . . . my friends."

"Very touching," said the queen. "But now you must choose. Tell us where they are—and go home. Or stay in the fungus pit till you die. Decide!"

"All right, I'll decide," he said. "But I'd like to whisper it to you."

"Oh, come closer," ordered the queen. "I don't have all day."

Lawrence slowly approached the queen and in one quick motion kicked her as hard as he could.

"There! That's what I decide," he yelled.

"Get him!" shouted Antentius.

"Run," said Bleato. "Run for your life!" Lawrence darted away into the astonished crowd. They made it through the crowd and into the empty tunnel.

"Which way?"

"That way, uphill will take us out," said Bleato. Before them, the tunnel curved and straightened and curved again.

"Can't you run any faster?" yelled Bleato. They could hear the guards in close pursuit.

"We're trapped," said Lawrence, coming to the end of a passage.

"In here," yelled Bleato, pointing to an opening Lawrence had not seen.

They came immediately face-to-face with several terrified nurses in a room filled with a thousand little white ovals.

"Pardon me, ladies," said Bleato. "We're here to eat your eggs." The nurses, screaming, ran to protect their eggs in a giant pit in the middle of the chamber. Suddenly, Antentius burst in behind them.

"The runt's with him," he yelled. "Seize them!"

"Jump," yelled Bleato.

And without a second thought Lawrence plunged into the pit of eggs. They quickly slithered down between them until they reached the bottom. It was an eerie sight looking at the ovals, the unborn ants clearly visible inside each egg.

"One day soon, these cute little things will be killing our soldiers, capturing our territory and raising havoc with our citizens. But now they're not such bad fellows," said Bleato.

Feeling his way through the eggs, Lawrence finally made his way across the bottom of the pit. They could hear the guards yelling to each other up above. They eased up the wall and Lawrence stuck his head out just enough for Bleato to climb up and peer over the top.

"There's a tunnel. Let's go."

The passageways were empty. They moved silently up, up, up until they saw the light from an opening leading out of the colony. It was heavily guarded.

"There must be ten of them," said Bleato.

"Well, we've come this far." Lawrence jumped up running and blew right by them. A moment later, they were out of the colony, running madly into the desert.

"Better run fast," said Bleato. "Instant death is just moments behind."

"Thanks for letting me know," replied Lawrence. "I had forgotten."

Suddenly, there were rocks on one side and a ditch on the other.

"Stop!" yelled Bleato. It was almost too late, but Lawrence dug in his heels and fell backwards. Slowly, he sat up and looked down. They were just inches from the edge of Rockface Cliff.

"Guess I went the wrong way," said Lawrence.

A warm breeze came up the side of the cliff and lifted the hair off his forehead. Suddenly, they heard shouting.

"Here they come," yelled Bleato, looking over his shoulder. "Can we get down?"

Lawrence eased to the edge and looked down. The height was dizzying. He could barely see the bottom.

"No, there's no place to climb down," he said. Again the wind came from below. This time it was so strong it blew Lawrence back from the edge. When he leaned back, the wind was still. But when he leaned over the edge, it was strong. Just down the cliff there was a giant barrel cactus, and in the middle of this cactus was a purple flower. He stared at it.

"I've got another idea," said Lawrence.

"Uh…whatever you have in mind, now would be a good time," pleaded Bleato, "because—"

"There they are!" yelled Antentius, as he came into sight leading a few hundred soldiers.

"Hold on," yelled Lawrence.

With Bleato on his shoulder, Lawrence slid over the edge and landed with a bump at the base of the barrel cactus.

"No offense, but isn't this a funny time to be observing our native plants?" said Bleato.

"Climb up to that flower," said Lawrence.

"First we slide off a cliff and now we have to climb up into the sharpest spines in the territory. This is going to be fun."

"No time to talk," said Lawrence. "Just go."

"Get down there and get them," yelled Antentius from above.

Lawrence reached the flower and spread the petals apart.

"Get in, Bleato. Quickly."

"It's a very pretty flower, Lawrence, really it is, but. . . ."

"Get in!" shouted Lawrence.

"All right, all right."

Three large red ants appeared. Lawrence quickly closed the petals behind Bleato and dropped down to the stem. He took hold and yanked and yanked and pulled and pulled until he thought his shoulder would pop out. But the stem wouldn't come out. He looked around for something to cut it with. Using his foot, Lawrence broke off a cactus needle. He turned the point toward the advancing red ants. "Stop!" he yelled. The soldiers stopped. Lawrence swung the point of the cactus needle into the flower stem and it cut clean through. He jumped through the petals and into the flower.

"Come on, come on," he said, but the wind had suddenly died and nothing happened. "Come on, come on."

"If I may ask, what's supposed to happen now?" said Bleato. "No doubt this is a lovely and fragrant place, but it's the Creenios were supposed to be getting away from—"

Several red ants got a hold of the stem and were shaking the flower, trying to get them out. Then the hot desert wind caught the flower and a moment later it started to rise.

"Hold on," yelled Lawrence. The flower rose just a little and stopped, because the red ants were still holding it.

"Don't let go," yelled Antentius. The wind got stronger, and the soldiers had to let go. The flower rose higher and higher, up the cliff, past Antentius. As the Creenio leader tried frantically to catch the flower with his antennas, it floated just past his reach. Bleato opened the petals.

"You know, we'd love to stay, really we would, but our calendar is so full these days that we just have to be on our way," he said.

"Stop them, stop them!" boomed Antentius.

But his soldiers were helpless. The flower caught a warm gust of air and floated higher and higher above the cliffs. Antentius and his red army were soon only tiny dots on the hillside below. Then the shifting wind sent them floating across the desert toward the mountains.

"We're up with the birds," shouted Bleato. For a while, he looked out between the petals and watched their flight. Then he sat back and looked at Lawrence for a long time in a strange way.

"It's true," he said.

"What's true?" replied Lawrence.

"The prophecy—it's true."

"Don't be ridiculous."

"No, it must be," said Bleato. "Just like our first queen, we were thrown off the cliffs and floated away. The prophecy is true."

"I can't save the Magyars. I can barely save myself," said Lawrence.

"The prophecy says that a foreigner will come in times of great trouble and help the colony survive. You're a foreigner, these are times of great trouble, no doubt about that, and now you've followed Queen Riadda off the cliffs and lived. This does not take a large brain to figure out."

"Yeah, well, who said anything about lived? Look down! Hold on! We're gonna hit!"

10

Lawrence quickly spread the petals, slid down the stem, and planted his feet firmly on the smooth round mountaintop. For a moment he stood there, looking out over the entire territory, holding the flower upright. Bleato opened the petals.

"We're on top of Mount Baldy," he said.

The wind picked up the flower and off they went again. Lawrence held onto the stem as they floated away.

"What are you doing?" said Bleato. "This is no time for acrobatics. Get back in here."

Lawrence settled back into the flower and smiled. "I'll be more careful from now on."

"How high can we go?" asked Bleato, taking a peak over the side.

"Who knows?"

The desert below them grew pink, then purple, then black, as the sun went down and then turned ghostly white as a full moon appeared. The night was warm and they floated silently between the hills, rising higher and higher.

"Lawrence, look!" Bleato shrieked suddenly. Lawrence, startled, thought they were about to hit something and jumped up. But they were still very high off the ground.

Bleato was beside himself. "Stars! Stars on the ground! Hundreds of them, thousands of them, on the ground! Look, look!" Bleato jumped up Lawrence's arm to get a better look from his shoulder.

Lawrence settled down softly between the petals and peered out. "Those aren't stars," he said sadly.

"Then what are they?" asked Bleato, mystified.

"Lights."

"What are lights?"

"Those are the lights from the city. That's where I live."

"You mean, that's where you're trying to get back to?"

"Yep."

"Oh," said Bleato, softly. "It's seems so close. Why not just float over and I'll drop you there?"

"It wouldn't be the same."

Neither of them spoke for a long while. They just floated over the town, over the lights, over the streets. The city opened up below them like a giant carpet of glimmering diamonds.

"There's my school," Lawrence exclaimed, pointing excitedly. "And the market. And the Capitol building. And the soccer fields. There's the mall. And the plaza."

"And I thought Magyar Hill was big," said Bleato. "It's like a thousand colonies all put together."

They floated a while longer. "Look down there. It's the road to my house," he exclaimed. The wind took them over a hill. Lawrence grew silent.

"What is it?" said Bleato.

"It's my house," he said. "There." He pointed below.

"What's a house?"

"It's like your colony," replied Lawrence. "Where I live."

"It's big. You must have a few thousand humans in there."

"No, just me and my mom and dad."

"There? You gotta be kidding me," said Bleato. "That big colony and only three of you?"

"Yep," said Lawrence. "And look, the lights are on."

Then, as if by magic, the flower made half a turn and floated down to about roof level. The back door opened and someone came out and stood on the porch.

"Mom," said Lawrence, but he knew she could not hear him. "Mom, it's me. I'm here. I'm right above you and I'm okay. I'll be back. I promise."

Suddenly, the wind shifted and they sailed over the house and back out of town into the hills.

"Your eyes are full of water again," said Bleato. "Very strange."

"I'll be okay," he replied, turning away.

All night they floated on, cradled by the soft wind. Then, as the sun came up over the Sangre de Cristo Mountains, they found themselves in a large valley spotted by cactus.

"Where are we?" said Lawrence, surveying the land-scape.

"Got me," replied Bleato. "Different territory, for sure."

All of a sudden, the wind that had been soft and steady all night died down, and they headed slowly toward the desert floor.

"Uh oh, we've got company," said Bleato, peering over the side.

Below, an army of ants was running to keep up with the descending flower.

"Who are they?" asked Lawrence.

Bleato shrugged. "Lots of colonies around here. Could be any of them."

"Are they friendly?"

"I doubt it," said Bleato. "They'll probably tear us apart when we land."

"That makes me feel better."

"The Creenios long ago conquered most of the colonies around here. They're probably good buddies with Antentius."

"Now that's a cheery thought," said Lawrence.

Their flower gondola landed with a jolt, stayed upright for a single moment, and then fell to one side, spilling Lawrence and Bleato out onto the ground. These black ants, jabbering in some language they could not understand, quickly made a circle around them. Lawrence tried to speak, but he couldn't be heard over the clamoring voices and snapping jaws. A thousand antennas waved over their heads.

The crowd suddenly parted and fell silent. A giant ant approached out of the crowd. The sight of this bizarre looking ant startled Lawrence at first and he almost burst out laughing. Had he not feared for his life, he might have. This ant walked with great airs, cocked his head to one side, and stuck out his lower lip in a very comic way. The little hairs on his head were plastered down and his moustache was parted in the middle and combed outward. He walked in massive bold strides, like a creature who knew his place, and his place was leader. As he got near, Lawrence thought that he smelled cologne like his father's, or at least something like it, coming off the ant.

The ant stopped and bent over them, making his inspection. The army awaited his words. The ant stepped back and turned to his soldiers.

"Prepare za table immediately," he said, in an accent so thick Lawrence could barely understand him. "We must have za feast."

"Uh oh, see what I told you," said Bleato. "We're the main course."

Hearing this, the giant ant wheeled and shook his head.

"On the contrary, you shall be za guests of honor." He extended his antenna in greeting. "I am General DeGaulle, leader of the Burgans. And I would be most delighted if you would join us at our table."

Lawrence and Bleato were so surprised they burst out laughing. Then they hurried to touch his antenna.

"We accept," said Bleato. "It is always better to eat than to be eaten."

The general roared with laughter and his troops joined in. "I love za little one. He iz so funny," he said.

In practically no time they were seated in front of a massive feast that stretched out before them on the hillside. But it was not what Lawrence had expected. This feast was not simply dead bugs warmed in the sun, the food Lawrence was getting used to. This was intricately prepared food, dishes, and concoctions, with sauces and herbs and spices. A dozen chefs were running from dish to dish, seeing to every last detail. Lawrence and Bleato were both astounded by such a display, and it must have shown on their faces.

"Ah, you like za roasted grasshopper au juniper?" said DeGaulle. "I had za chef prepare it for you specially. Would you like to know how it iz prepared? Zen I will tell you. It iz roasted in the za sun for one morning on a flat stone with sage and wild grasses. Zen za chef she makes za sauce from the juniper berry, and it iz poured over za grasshopper and voila, magnifique! We also have za moth with piñon sauce, centipede with sage, and many other delicacies. Please begin."

Without hesitation, Lawrence dug in. Grasshopper meat no longer repulsed him, and besides, he was hungry. It tasted wonderful. The general smiled broadly, as Lawrence nodded in appreciation.

"I'd like to try the moth with piñon sauce," said Bleato.

"Ah, go ahead, my leetle friend," said DeGaulle. "Come, let us all begin."

Seated next to a lovely rock garden, Lawrence ate everything offered to him. Most of the time he did not know what he was eating, and did not ask. The officers laughed and told jokes and they quickly took a liking to Lawrence and Bleato. They even teased him about his size.

"Sure, sure, go ahead," said Bleato, "but if I get one of you on the battlefield, you're spider meat."

This comeback sent the officers into tailspins of laughter and they drank to his health.

"Have zome wine," said DeGaulle.

"You have wine?" asked Lawrence.

"Of course we have wine. We are in za territory of Queen Ant-Marie in the Colony of Burgans—so it would be uncivilized not to have wine."

"I'm not old enough to have wine," said Lawrence.

"No wine? Zat iz the most ridiculous thing I've ever heard. Try zome. It iz made from the piñon berry. You will like it."

Not wanting to offend his host, Lawrence took a sip. It tasted like grape juice, except bitter. He nodded vigorously and drank some more.

"Do you mind if I ask you a question?" Lawrence said to DeGaulle.

"But of course."

"How did you know who we were, when we landed, I mean?"

"Ah, zat iz za question, iz it not?" answered DeGaulle. "But I shall tell you because you are my guest here. We have spies. We know everything zat goes on in all za territories."

"And you heard about us?"

"But of course, you are famous now. I knew when you first arrived, with your friend who joined za Creenios. Not a good choice on his part. I know zat you joined the Magyars. A good choice, but you came at a very bad time, I'm afraid. Za flood has destroyed Magyar Hill and the Creenios took zere soldiers as prisoners. You escaped with Sephea. I do not know where she iz hiding, although I can guess. I also know zat Antentius has taken a serious dislike to you, my friend, and zat iz not a good thing."

"I'm afraid you're right," replied Lawrence.

"When I saw za cactus flower, floating above, I knew it had to be you. And as for Bleato, everyone knows za little soldier."

"I am not a soldier," said Bleato. "But one day, I might be."

"Zat iz right, do not give up, leetle one," said DeGaulle. "Zome day you may be za bravest soldier in za entire valley."

"Are you going to send us back?" Bleato demanded.

"Never," said DeGaulle. "Za Creenios are our enemies."

"Good, pass the stink bug," said Bleato, digging in.

"You are very lucky," DeGaulle continued. "There are many colonies around us and each has been conquered by the Creenios. If you had landed in any one of those, you would be on your way back to Creenio Colony by now—or worse."

"Thank you," said Lawrence, quietly. "I don't think I could go back there."

"Oh, it iz nothing, my friend. We hate the Creenios too. They are our sworn enemies. We have fought many wars with zem, and will fight many more."

"Will you help us fight zem, I mean them?" Lawrence blurted out. The officers fell silent and DeGaulle frowned. Lawrence immediately knew he had blundered.

DeGaulle waved his antenna to break the tension. "Come, it iz time to meet za queen. I will take you now."

Lawrence and Bleato scrambled to their feet and followed him into the rock garden. They went down a little hill and suddenly were soon surrounded by every conceivable cactus—pinchushions, rainbows, barrels and hedgehogs, and a giant pineapple cactus as the crown jewel. Narrow paths lined with small white stones meandered through the garden. Tiny, slow-moving streams connected a series of still pools and desert flowers bloomed along their banks in great patches of white and purple and yellow.

"Ah, you like my gardens, I see," said a soft, musical voice from behind them. Lawrence turned to face a large female, unlike any ant he had seen before. This queen was slender, delicate, almost pretty. She had long, shapely legs, a thin waist, and a perfectly balanced upper torso. Her soft and perfectly oval eyes glittered in the sunlight. When they came to rest on Lawrence, he melted. Her voice was like beautiful music. Every move of her head and body seemed to be choreographed, and every gesture had a studied grace and charm. Lawrence bowed to her. She smiled at him.

"May I present Queen Ant-Marie," said DeGaulle. "Your majesty, may I present Lawrence, a soldier in the army of the Magyars."

"Nice to meet you," Lawrence stammered.

"And I am enchanted to make your acquaintance," she cooed.

"And I'm Bleato," said a squeaky voice.

"How cuuuuuttttttte!" exclaimed the queen. "Come, sit on my shoulder while we tour the gardens."

"Royalty loves me," whispered Bleato, as he hopped up onto the queen's shoulder.

"Is everything all right for you there?" asked the queen, smiling.

"You bet, Queenie," said Bleato. "Ready when you are."

The queen then dismissed her attendants who had followed her into the garden and led Lawrence and DeGaulle along the paths. The garden, an enchanted paradise, was an extension of the queen's beauty. She spoke of it as she walked, with such love and affection that Lawrence saw that it was part of her. At last, she invited them to sit down in the shade.

"I assume you are on a diplomatic mission from the Magyars," she began.

Lawrence was caught off guard, but Bleato nodded to him vigorously from the queen's shoulder, so he said: "Yes, your majesty."

"May I know your purpose?" she inquired.

"As you know, your majesty, the Magyars have fallen on hard times," Bleato cut in. "After many generations,

Magyar Hill has been overrun by the Creenios and now faces extinction."

"The Creenios will not rest until they control every colony in the valley," said Queen Ant-Marie, a weariness in her voice.

"We would like your help to fight off the Creenios and rescue the Magyar queen, Queen Andulusia, from the red colony," said Lawrence.

The queen sighed, and then spoke. "Lawrence, you are obviously a worthy soldier, but you are also a foreigner, so I must share something. We have been in this valley, fighting the Creenios, for thousands of generations. We shall be here fighting them for thousands more. When we fight, it must be on our terms, not theirs. We fight only when we have a good chance at victory. Is that not right, General DeGaulle?"

"Yes, I am afraid it iz just so, your majesty."

"At the moment I do not see any chance of victory," she said. "However, if that were to change. . . ."

"If you do not help us, I think we are doomed," said Lawrence.

"Now is not the right time, but we shall see how things turn out," she replied.

"But you shall be our guests!" said DeGaulle.

"Do not despair, Lawrence," said the queen. "DeGaulle here has asked my permission to train you to fight like one of our soldiers, and I have granted my consent."

"Before you leave here," DeGaulle exclaimed, "you will be za most feared foreigner in the desert. We shall begin za training in za morning."

The next morning, after a good night's rest in one of the queen's own antechambers, five impressive-looking officers collected Lawrence and marched him to the Parade Ground.

DeGaulle was waiting. He bowed deeply. "Today we shall kill you many times," said DeGaulle, with a wry smile. "But it iz nothing to take personally."

"I understand," replied Lawrence, preparing himself.

DeGaulle ordered the first officer to attack him and before Lawrence could make a single move the ant had him down in the stinging position.

"Dead!" shouted DeGaulle. "Next!"

DeGaulle sent the next officer, and the next and the next.

"Dead," he called each time. "You have much to learn," said DeGaulle.

"I need my sword," said Lawrence, getting a bit discouraged.

"And what iz zat?"

"It's my weapon," he replied. "You have your stinger, I have my sword. It's long and pointy at one end and extremely sharp. The Creenios took it from me."

"A sword you say, hmm. . . ." said DeGaulle. He walked to the edge of the Grounds and broke off a cactus needle. He touched the sharp point.

"That'll do fine," said Lawrence. "Now I can fight." He placed it in his hand.

"One moment," said DeGaulle. "Here, use two." He broke off another needle and placed it in Lawrence's left hand. Lawrence didn't know what to make of it.

"I'm right-handed," he said. "I don't need this."

"But you do, my friend," said DeGaulle. "I have a stinger, jaws, two antennas, and mandibles. All for fighting. You need more than one sword."

"I can't learn to use this," Lawrence.

"Zen you shall die," replied DeGaulle.

"That kind of ends that conversation, I'd say," said Bleato.

For three hot days and well into the nights, Lawrence fought with his two swords, under the watchful eye of DeGaulle. At first, the second sword hung loosely, uselessly, by his side. But slowly he began to bring it into play, first to parry, then to thrust. By the third day when the officers lined up the piñon berries for target practice, Lawrence could slash the berry with either sword. On the fourth day, DeGaulle once again sent his soldiers against Lawrence, but this time he turned them all back. Not one officer could kill him.

"As I expected, I have done a magnificent job with you, my friend. You will be za most feared fighter in za valley," said DeGaulle.

"What about me?" asked Bleato.

"Ah, you are already most feared," replied DeGaulle, and the soldiers laughed.

Several days later, as Lawrence and Bleato prepared to leave, the entire colony came out onto the Parade Grounds to see them off. The queen presented Lawrence with two new swords as a going-away gift. They were longer than any sword he had used, with points so sharp they could cut his finger. The broad side was flat and smooth, but the edge was sharp as a razor blade. These were fine, dangerous swords.

"Where did you get these?" asked Lawrence, astonished by the craftsmanship.

"An old friend of yours made them—a termite."

"Gusteffes! He saved my life when I first got here."

"He was delighted you were still alive," said DeGaulle. "He sends his regards."

Lawrence kneeled and kissed the queen's foreleg, but Bleato climbed up and gave her a peck on the cheek, giving the troops a good laugh.

"Thank you for everything," said Lawrence.

"Good luck against the Creenios," said the queen, "and we hope you find your turquoise stone."

"How did you know about that?" he asked, surprised.

"Our spies tell us everything," said DeGaulle, smiling.

"Keep in touch, my friend," said Queen Ant-Marie. "Come to see us any time."

Lawrence and Bleato quickly walked to the top of the pass and turned. Tens of thousands of forelegs danced in the air, waving good-bye.

They started walking. By midday, they had reached the Great Arroyo.

"It is fastest to go straight up the arroyo," said Lawrence.

"It's crazy," said Bleato. "It could rain."

"Nonsense, there's not a cloud in the sky."

"All right, but I warned you."

It was hard going. They had to descend steep sand cliffs, climb over driftwood, go round huge clumps of dried grass. They made slow progress. Lawrence felt the sun burning his shoulders through his ripped shirt. His arms and legs were now almost the color of chocolate. The sand penetrated his shoes and burned his toes and there was no water to be found, not even little puddles from the last rainfall. Water disappeared quickly after a rainstorm in the desert, but he didn't realize how quickly. They kept to the middle of the arroyo.

"What was that?" said Bleato, stopping to listen.

"I didn't hear anything," replied Lawrence.

"Thunder."

"There aren't even any clouds, Bleato."

"It's going to rain."

"How do you know?"

"I always know. It's my neck again."

"All right, we'll head for the side," Lawrence said wearily, not convinced. But moments later, a tremendous thunderclap shook the mountains.

"We've got to get out of here," screamed Bleato.

They ran for the side of the streambed, but Lawrence could see that it was going to take a long time. "I know, I know, I'm going as fast as I can," he yelled.

The clouds quickly moved in. The sky, which had been bright blue a moment before, now grew dark with storm clouds. It started to rain lightly. It wasn't much at first; it even felt good to cool off. But it grew heavier by the minute. Soon the raindrops pelted them, making it hard to keep going. The sand quickly turned into a giant mud pit. Then giant thunder exploded and there was a tremendous cloudburst. The water came down in sheets.

A low rumbling sound was heard, up the arroyo.

"What's that?" yelled Lawrence.

"It's coming," said Bleato.

11

The wall of churning water crashed over their heads and sucked them under. But then, just as quickly, they were thrust to the surface, gasping for air.

"Here we go again," said Bleato, frantically hanging on as best he could.

Down they went, spinning around and around, and then were shot up again. A moment later, the water sucked them under and pinned Lawrence against a sand bar and then ripped him loose and flipped him out of the water.

"I'm sure glad we walked in the middle of the arroyo," yelled Bleato, just as they got pulled under again.

Lawrence spotted a dark object just overhead—a piece of driftwood.

"Grab on," yelled Lawrence, as they broke the surface.

"You grab on," replied Bleato. "I'm holding onto you, re-member?"

They climbed aboard and rode the driftwood down river like a surfboard. Lawrence found that by moving his weight from side-to-side he could steer the craft to avoid rocks and sand bars.

"What's that ahead?" yelled Bleato. "Watch out!"

But too late. They plunged over a waterfall and Lawrence lost his grip on the driftwood while in midair. Down they went and landed with a great splash. But the large pool at the base of the waterfall was amazingly calm and they were able to swim to the edge and climb out onto a sand wall.

"Now there's a surprise," said Bleato. "We're still alive."

"Come on, let's get out of here," said Lawrence.

They clawed their way up, loose sand giving way in their hands, until they reached the top, exhausted. The rain was still coming down hard, pitting the sand around Lawrence. Now that they were out of danger, Lawrence felt the bitter cold and started to shiver violently.

"Are you okay?" asked Bleato. "You don't look too good."

"Need to get . . . out of . . . the rain," he replied.

"Under here."

Bleato led him to half a piñon shell wedged into the sand, probably dropped by a bird. It made a perfect shelter. They ducked under. It was dry underneath. The rain made a deafening sound on the shell, which made their ears ring, but they were just glad to get out of the cold and wet. Lawrence sat down—fell down, actually—against the side of the shell and took several deep breaths but couldn't stop from shaking.

"You'll be okay," said Bleato, with a yawn, "after we get some rest."

They both fell asleep and when they awoke, it was sunny outside. The sky was bright blue against the Sangre de Cristo Mountains, clouds bright white and puffy, rising up to the heavens. Lawrence eased himself from under the shell and stretched.

Bleato, bleary-eyed, soon joined him on the plateau. At the edge of the sand bar, they peered down into the still pool below. It was so clear they could see every rock on the bottom.

Lawrence was amused at the reflections in the water: a wild boy, with his clothes in tatters, sandy blond hair a tangled mess, face and body hard like something of the desert, and next to this wild looking thing was a tiny ant peering down.

"That's us," said Lawrence. "Down in the pool."

"That's me?" stammered Bleato, amazed at his own reflection.

"I look pretty scary," said Lawrence.

Quickly he stripped off his clothes.

"You can take off your skin?" exclaimed Bleato, dumbfounded. "You foreigners are weird."

Lawrence dived into the pool and swam to the middle, laughing.

"Are you crazy? What are you doing?" yelled Bleato.

"Swimming."

"What's that?"

"Come in and see."

"Ants don't normally go into large pools of water, unless chased by Creenios, of course," said Bleato.

"Just jump! I'll catch you," said Lawrence.

"Oh, why not?" yelled Bleato, launching himself into the air and landing with a tiny splash. He sank right to the bottom. Lawrence had to dive down and bring him up. "Now that . . .that . . . that was really fun," said Bleato, sputtering and coughing. "Remind me to do this again some time real soon."

They spent the rest of the day swimming and playing on the beach. Lawrence skipped rocks while Bleato stayed in the shallow area trying to learn to swim.

"How do I look?" he yelled.

"Like an ant trying to swim," replied Lawrence.

"That's what I am."

Soon they were hungry and gathered berries from the nearby branches and had a feast. By now it was late afternoon and they sat in the shade of a sage plant to avoid the heat.

"Lawrence."

"Yes, Bleato."

"Will you promise me something?"

"What?"

Bleato hesitated. "Stay here, please. Don't go back to where you came from."

"Bleato, you know I. . . ."

"You won't have to worry about food and all that. You're already a soldier, which is more than I can say for myself. You can be a Magyar forever."

Lawrence sighed.

"You see," Bleato continued, "No one has ever treated me like you do. Everyone else treats me like a runt. Please stay."

"I might," said Lawrence. "We'll see."

Lawrence picked him up. "Bleato, you're as good as any of them." Bleato smiled and closed his eyes and they drifted off to sleep.

At sundown they awoke and started back toward the Caves. They traveled safely under cover of darkness and by sunup had their destination in sight.

The Caves were alive. There were many more soldiers than before—a real army preparing to take the field. Soldiers were forming up in the rocky bowl, as the leaders emerged from Sephea's cave and joined up with their forces.

"When we left, this was a sleepy place," said Bleato. "What happened?"

"Word went out," said a passing soldier. "And they came."

Sephea came up to them and greeted them happily, glad to see them alive. "We put out the word that any colony wanting to rebel against the Creenios should join us here, and a dozen armies came," she said. "We march soon."

"March? Where are we going?" asked Bleato.

"Why, to defeat the Creenios, of course," replied Sephea.

"Seph, have you gone nuts? We've just come from Creenio colony. Even with all these soldiers, you are still outnumbered five to one."

"But we are fighting for freedom," said Sephea quietly, and off she went.

"Oh, I'm sure Antentius is shaking right now," said Bleato.

"How many soldiers does he have?" asked Lawrence.

"Oh, only about six hundred thousand. But we're fighting for freedom, so hey, why not, right?"

"It looks bad, then?"

"Not for you. Nobody said you have to fight," said Bleato.

"You forget two things," replied Lawrence. "One, I'm a Magyar soldier, so I have to fight, and two, they've got the turquoise stone, and I need it—"

Lawrence stopped himself, but it was too late. He saw the recognition in Bleato's eyes, and the little ant turned away quickly.

"Let the fighting begin," said Pantara, coming up behind them. "You two march with me, you got that?"

"We're with you," said Lawrence, with a smile.

At dusk they made their way over the pass and onto Cactus Butte. Soon the moon was full and they could see easily. By dawn they had reached the far side of the butte and started down into Centipede Valley, stretching out as far as they could see. It was midmorning before they reached Crow's Overlook, a hill at the end of the Great Sandy Plain where Creenio territory began.

In the distance was the towering red ant colony. Not surprisingly, Creenio spies had done their work and Antentius was there, greeting them across the Great Sandy Plain. But the battle did not start right away as expected. Antentius sent a messenger and arranged to meet Sephea, who went down with a party that included Pantara and Lawrence and Bleato to meet him face-to-face.

His giant red face awaited them. He looked them over, then laughed. "I'll tell you what I'll do," he said to Sephea. "You are a ridiculous-looking army, and I could crush you at any moment. But there may be a way to avoid a battle."

"I'm listening," said Sephea.

"I'll let you have your queens and your colony back—"

"That's all we want."

"But there's something I want," growled Antentius. "I want the foreigner."

"You want Lawrence?" said Sephea, blinking in confusion.

"You can't have him," called out Bleato.

"The queen wants him," said Antentius.

"He's a soldier in our army," squealed Bleato. "You can't have him."

"Bleato, I'll handle this," said Sephea.

"You can't let them have him!"

"Antentius, he is a soldier in our army," said Sephea. "We cannot give him up."

"He is no soldier. He is a foreigner. I say, hand him over and I'll call off my troops. Otherwise you will be annihilated."

Lawrence stepped forward. "Are you telling us that if I come with you you'll give them back their queen and colony?"

"Yes."

"Why? What's the real reason?" asked Sephea.

"Because he wants to use the power of the turquoise against us, and he needs Lawrence," yelled Bleato. "That's why."

"No bargain is easy," said Antentius. "Give me the foreigner and live. Or hold him back and die."

"You'll free all the slaves?" asked Lawrence.

"Yes. All of them."

"And guarantee them free passage back to Magyar Hill?"

"Yes."

There was long pause as Lawrence looked Antentius directly in the eyes. "Then I'll go."

"You can't!" said Bleato, sinking to the ground.

"Now it becomes clear," said Sephea, sadly. "This is the meaning of the prophecy. I just didn't think you'd have to give up your life to save us."

"You would do the same for the colony, wouldn't you?" Lawrence responded.

"Yes, but. . . ."

"But I am not a Magyar? Is that what you're thinking?" He smiled. "Antentius, take me—and let them go."

"Seize him!" growled the leader.

Suddenly, pushing two soldiers aside, Tony elbowed his way to where they were standing. "It's a trick. It's a trick," he yelled. "They are going to massacre everyone. Run, run."

They were all so astonished that no one moved. But then Antentius flew into a rage and ordered his soldiers to take Tony away. Then Antentius with one leap grabbed Lawrence around the neck. But Tony instantly plowed into Antentius, and they all fell to the ground. Lawrence struggled free.

"Fall back, fall back," yelled Sephea.

"You will pay for this with your lives," yelled Antentius, heading back to join his armies.

Bleato jumped onto Lawrence's back and they quickly made their way to Crow's Overlook, where their armies awaited them.

Sephea quickly divided the army into four fighting units. They slowly marched down onto the Great Sandy Plain, where the entire Creenio army was waiting, assured of victory.

Sephea trembled. "Oh, Homeron, wherever you are, I need you now. If you can hear my call, I could use a little help. . . ."

Her troops were in a trance, frightened by the sight of so many red ants coming towards them and the giant dust ball rising up as they came.

"All right," she said, simply, "let's go win our freedom."

This broke the trance, and the soldiers scurried off to battle stations. Lawrence joined the fighting unit under Pantara's command. Their job was to capture and hold Windstruck Mesa. They had to get there before the Creenios.

It was slow going and many of their soldiers were caught and killed by the red soldiers sent to slow them down. But Pantara reached the top and took control, giving orders quietly and calmly. They took up defensive positions to meet the Creenio advance. Soldiers from the other colonies, Cadolians, Quittans, Molekkers, and others, took up rear positions. As the red army came up the hill, there looked to be no stopping it. There were thousands of them, relentlessly advancing. On top, Pantara had only a few hundred soldiers.

Then Lawrence noticed loose rocks about his feet. He turned to Pantara. "Roll the rocks down the hillside," he yelled over the noise of the battle. "These rocks can be our weapons."

Pantara didn't understand, as ants never use weapons.

"We'll kill them with the rocks!" shouted Bleato, who understood immediately.

Pantara looked confused. "I'll show you," said Lawrence. He went and got a rock, cocked his arm, and flung it down the hill. It hit a dozen ants and knocked them out.

"Now that I like," said Pantara, as he gave the order. Moments later a hundred rocks were brought to the edge. Lawrence was now in command. He ran from rock to rock, looking for just the right one to push. Then he put his shoulder against it and, with help from the soldiers, down it rolled, taking out more and more Creenios.

The red ants had never seen anything like it. The Magyars could see the fear in the eyes of their enemies, and it made them bold. After each rock a hundred or so Magyars would race down the hillside and attack the fleeing, terrified red ants. The battle had turned.

"Look, they're retreating," said Lawrence. "We've won."

"Not yet. All battles stop in the heat of the day," said Sephea.

"They'll be back when it cools off," said Bleato.

"Then come on," Lawrence yelled, to Bleato. "We've got work to do."

12

They arrived at Burgan Colony in the heat of the day, and the guards took them directly to see the queen and General DeGaulle.

"Ah, Lawrence, what a surprise to see you again," said Queen Ant-Marie. "Tell us what has happened. I love news."

"Your majesty, we have been fighting the Creenios," Lawrence said, breathlessly.

"And how iz it going?" asked DeGaulle.

"At the moment they are in retreat, but. . . ."

"But what?" said the queen, puzzled.

"Their numbers are too great. We are going to lose when they return," said Lawrence flatly, "unless you come and fight with us."

There was a long pause. DeGaulle shrugged. "We have told you, Lawrence, that we cannot fight the Creenios every time someone else fights a war wiz zem."

"But all will be lost," Lawrence pleaded.

"I'm sorry," said the queen, bowing her head.

"Your majesty and General DeGaulle," said Bleato, gathering his courage, "if you do not come to our aid, your colony will be conquered by the Creenios."

"And why iz zat?" asked DeGaulle, surprised by Bleato's confidence.

"First a little geography. Your colony is situated between Mount Baldy and Spider Bluff. The Creenios can attack you by coming over Eagle Nest Pass and going by Mount Baldy, but they can't attack from Spider Bluff because it's Magyar territory, or I should say it *was* Magyar territory."

"I cannot argue with zat," said DeGaulle.

"Now, if the Creenios control Magyar Hill, they also control Atalaya Peak, and so the entire plain between the peak and your colony is now exposed. Is that not right?"

"Absolutely correct," acknowledged the queen.

"The arroyo, which up to now has been controlled by the Magyars, will now be in Creenio hands, so your entire flank is exposed. Attacks will come from one end of the valley to the other, unless the Magyars are restored."

"This could be true," said the queen.

"And to make things even more perilous, the Piñon Hillside will belong to the Creenios, which means they can attack— from above! In short, after the Magyars, you will most certainly be attacked next. And despite your great army, you won't be able to stop them. No colony could defend all those points for long. So if you don't come to our aid now, then in no time at all Antentius will have his fat gaster on your rock garden and the only wine you'll be drinking is from the berries brought into his fungus pit."

"Hmmm, Bleato has become a very effective diplomat, I see," said the queen.

"And let's say you did hold out for a while," Bleato continued. "The Creenios will hold most of the valley, so you will not be able to gather food. That means less food, and that means fewer eggs and fewer soldiers. The Creenios can wait. Your army will be weak and they will attack."

DeGaulle rubbed his jaw with his foreleg. "Interesting," he said.

"This does present a new situation," said the queen.

"Your majesty, if I may say so, the time to save your colony is now," Bleato said.

Queen Ant-Marie and DeGaulle excused themselves to talk it over in a far-off corner of the rock garden. Several officers joined them.

"Do you think it worked?" said Bleato, waiting impatiently.

"Not a clue," replied Lawrence. "But you know something, Bleato, no one could have said it better."

"We have one question," said Queen Ant-Marie, suddenly returning. "If we help you and are victorious over the Creenios, who will control all za territory that we capture?"

"As a representative of the Magyars, I can offer you the territory from Eagle Nest Pass to Spider Bluff," Bleato replied immediately.

"Will you include Mount Baldy?"

That will be yours too," Bleato readily agreed.

The queen nodded at DeGaulle. "What do you say, General?" she asked.

"I shall lead za soldiers into the battle myself, your majesty," he replied. "And we shall win zee great victory, or my name iz not General DeGaulle."

In only moments, the entire Burgan army was on the march, Lawrence and Bleato out front with DeGaulle. As they passed through Spider Bluff, huge hairy tarantulas, black widows and other desert spiders looked on in amazement at this tremendous army of ants on the way to battle. They were across the arroyo in record time and soon gathered at the top of Eagle Nest Pass.

"Soldiers of Queen Ant-Marie," shouted DeGaulle. "Today will be a glorious day in our history. You shall win za battle against our sworn enemies, za Creenios." His soldiers roared. "Za Creenios want to take our liberty, our equality, and our wine!" he shouted. "We can't have zat, can we?"

"No," roared the soldiers.

"Onward to battle!"

It had cooled off by now and the battle was raging again on the Great Sandy Plain. The Burgan army poured down Eagle Nest Pass and attacked the Creenio army with terrific force. Antentius, taken by surprise, turned his army to fight them, but now was caught between the two forces. The Burgans and the Magyars ants soon cut the Creenio army into sections and surrounded them.

"Fools! Cowards! Fight them," yelled Antentius helplessly, but the Burgan army was too much for them and they scurried off into the desert.

But Antentius stood his ground, furious at being deserted by his troops. No matter how many soldiers came at him, he killed them all.

"I shall kill your queen," he shouted, heading back to Creenio Colony. The Magyars tried to stop him, but he moved too fast and killed too many. As he reached the entrance to the colony, Lawrence was waiting for him, swords ready.

Antentius laughed. "I should have killed you long ago, but it will be my pleasure to do so now," he said, defiantly. Lawrence eased over into a flat sandy patch, poised for battle.

"Jump off and run into the rocks," he whispered to Bleato. "No reason for both of us to die."

"Lawrence, please, let me fight. Let me be a soldier. I finally have my chance."

Lawrence sighed, his eyes on his adversary. "All right, but stay down."

Antentius moved in, ready for battle.

"I order you to surrender," said Lawrence, his voice shaking.

"Oh, he'll for sure go for that," said Bleato.

"Surrender?" said Antentius. "I will kill you instead. You and that worthless little runt."

He came at Lawrence with jaws snapping, antennas waving, mandibles closing rapidly. Lawrence jumped to one side, barely avoiding the mandibles, and rolled free.

"I see the foreigner is faster," said Antentius. "But can he fight?"

"He'll come over the top and try to sting you," whispered Bleato. "Dive down when he comes, roll over, and stab him from below."

"Oh, that sounds easy," said Lawrence. "No problem."

Antentius came just the way Bleato had said he would. Lawrence rolled onto his back and drove his sword up into the red ant's abdomen. Antentius let out a gasp and fell back, but the wound was only skin deep.

"I see the foreigner can fight," said Antentius, with a sneer. "Now let's see how he dies."

"He's coming low and fast," yelled Bleato. "Watch out."

With a quick movement, Antentius had his leg. Lawrence screamed out. In pain and anger, he raised his sword and brought it down on the red ant's back. Antentius fell back, but immediately regained his balance and came at Lawrence, grabbing him with his long forearms. One sword spun out of Lawrence's hand. Antentius pinned him to a rock, the wicked mandibles wrapped around his neck, cutting off his breath.

"Use the other sword," yelled Bleato.

Antentius was positioning his stinger for the death sting. Lawrence could only stare in horror. Suddenly, Bleato leaped onto Antentius and bit down hard on his ear. Antentius howled and with one mighty swipe of his foreleg flung Bleato against a rock. The little ant hit the rock and slid down, motionless. His arms now free, Lawrence swung his sword and chopped off one antenna close to his head. Antentius staggered back.

Inflamed at seeing Bleato's lifeless body, Lawrence charged the giant ant and drove his sword into his side. A gaping wound opened. Antentius staggered, collapsed, and rolled to one side. He could not move. Lawrence walked calmly up to him, looked down, and raised his sword. Antentius looked up at him defiantly.

Even now, even as he is about to die, he is brave, thought Lawrence. I must kill him. It is the law of the desert. He slowly brought his sword over his head.

"Stop!" yelled a voice from above. "If you kill Antentius, I shall kill your queen," hissed Queen Natoria as the Creenio guards brought out the Magyar Queen, Andulusia.

Lawrence froze, his sword held high.

"I shall make an exchange," said Queen Natoria. "Your queen for Antentius."

"What about Magyar Hill?" asked Sephea.

"You can have it. I will set all the colonies free. You shall have everything, but give me back Antentius."

DeGaulle stepped forward. "Lawrence, it iz up to you," he said. "You have beaten Antentius in battle. You may kill him. It iz the law of za desert."

Lawrence slowly lowered his weapon. "I accept your terms," he said, stepping back.

The Creenios released Queen Andulusia and she was escorted away from the colony by Magyar soldiers, as DeGaulle knelt over the lifeless Bleato.

"I'm afraid your leetle friend is gone," he said, sadly.

"Bleato!" yelled Lawrence, coming to his side. "He's dead." Lawrence felt the tears coming and this time there was no stopping them. "He didn't deserve to die. He saved my life."

Lawrence gently held the little ant in his arms, as Sephea peered over his shoulder.

"I was going to ask the queen to make him a soldier in the army," said Sephea.

"Really?" said Bleato, his eyes snapping open. "That's good, 'cause I'm feeling much better."

"You're alive!" yelled Lawrence.

"Bleato," said Queen Andulusia, "due to your courage in battle, I hereby commission you as a soldier in the army of Magyar Hill."

"A soldier? Do you mean it?" he replied.

"It is done," said the queen. "From today you are a soldier in my Royal Guard."

"A soldier? In the Queen's own guard? What can I say? I accept, that's what I say. A soldier at last!"

A thought suddenly seized Lawrence. Now I can go home, he said to himself.

He looked around for Queen Natoria and spotted her on a small rise in front of the colony, watching as her guards carried Antentius back into the colony.

"Go ahead, talk to her," said Bleato, reading his mind. "You can go. I'll be all right."

"Your majesty," he said, approaching her, "about my turquoise stone. . . ."

"Oh, yes, the stone," she said, smiling. "You would be wanting it now, I suppose."

"If you don't mind, I'd like to go home," Lawrence replied.

"I wish I could give it to you, Lawrence, but you see I don't actually have it."

Lawrence was stunned. "But you said—"

"We told you we had it so you would tell us where Sephea was hiding, but we never had it," said the queen. "I'm sorry."

"Then where is it?" asked Lawrence.

"I don't know for certain, but I have a pretty good idea." She looked over at DeGaulle.

"You?" said Lawrence. "You have it?"

"Yes, my friend, I have it," answered DeGaulle. "I have had it all along."

"Why didn't you tell me?"

"Because we needed you," he replied. "The prophecy says a foreigner would come and save us. You were that foreigner, my friend. Until your work was done, we could not let you go. But now—well, that's another story."

And then DeGaulle gave the signal with a flourish and over the hill poured hundreds of soldiers carrying the turquoise stone on their backs. They carefully placed it down in the sand

and stepped back. Both Magyars and Creenios, believing it to be magic, gathered around to touch it.

"You have done well as a soldier and member of our colony," said Queen Andulusia. "You may stay with us if you like."

"Thank you," said Lawrence politely. "But I have to go home."

"Then we shall give you a hero's farewell," she replied, smiling.

The troops cheered him as Lawrence, with Bleato on his shoulder, made his way to the stone.

"Hey, I'm a soldier now, so make way," shouted Bleato to the crowd.

"Oh, what have we done," said Sephea, in amusement. "You're impossible."

"Too late, the royal will is done," replied Bleato.

Lawrence reached the stone and then turned to address the army. "I enjoyed meeting all of you. Thank you for making me a soldier in your army. Thank you for everything."

"We are glad you came to our territory," said Queen Andulusia.

A guard ran up carrying both of his swords. Taking them, Lawrence dropped to one knee and offered one to the queen. She smiled and accepted it graciously. Then Lawrence turned and presented his second sword to DeGaulle.

"No, no, my friend," replied DeGaulle. "Keep it as a memento. You must take zomething to remember us with." Lawrence smiled and tucked the sword firmly under his belt.

"Well, here goes," he said, and placed his hand on the stone. "But wait! I almost forgot. Where's Tony?"

"He fought with the Creenios," Sephea reminded him, with a frown. "Why take him back?"

"We'll feed him to the spiders," said Bleato.

"No, I must take him back," said Lawrence. "He warned us of the trap. I'll take him back."

"We will find him then," agreed the queen. She ordered her scouts to begin a search.

While they waited, Sephea came up and said quietly, "Good-by, Lawrence, thank you for coming and . . . saving us."

"Sephea, I didn't do it, you did. Just like Homeron said you would. You saved Magyar Hill." She put her antenna up and Lawrence touched it.

"Will you come back sometime?" asked Bleato.

"If you need me, I'll try," he replied.

"You know, I wouldn't be a soldier now if you hadn't come here," said Bleato. "I won't forget."

Suddenly the guards yelled, "We've found the other foreigner." They hauled Tony onto the sandy patch. "We found him hiding in the rocks," said the guard. "He's afraid we're going to kill him, that's why he's shaking so much."

"Get up, Tony," said Lawrence. "We're going home."

"Home?" stammered Tony. "We're going home?"

"Come on, stand here with me. Put your hand on the stone," Lawrence said simply. "We'd like to go home now, please."

Instantly, the ground became a blur, trees shrank, the sand shot away from them like they were being launched in a rocket. The wind howled, mountains spun, the world became a blast of sound and color. Lawrence quickly covered his ears to keep his eardrums from splitting and closed his eyes. Then, abruptly, it was dead still.

Lawrence was almost too afraid to open his eyes. But then his eyes snapped open and he found himself on a hillside covered with piñon trees—and the trees were regular size. Below them was the arroyo, just as he had left it. And the mountains were now only hills again. Tony clutched Lawrence's leg, his eyes shut tight.

"Look where we are," said Lawrence. "We're home. Let's go."

The aspens on the mountains above were coming into full bloom, their green leaves gently moving in the light breeze. The cloudless sky was a rich deep blue. It was hot, but Lawrence, with Tony a few steps behind, felt good walking on familiar territory. Soon the sun dropped behind Atalaya Peak and the valley turned crimson and then purple. The air was still and there was not a sound to be heard.

13

Lawrence woke with a start. It was dark and smelled of coffee. For a few moments he had no idea where he was. Then he slowly sat up and looked around. And then it all came back to him.

This was Dennis's cabin. He had been asleep.

Dennis had two breakfast plates on the table with fry bread and beans. It smelled good. The Navajo motioned for Lawrence to join him. Wrapping himself in the Indian blanket to keep warm, he eased up and sat at the table. But he did not eat.

"Was it all a dream?" asked Lawrence.

"Maybe, maybe not," said Dennis, with a knowing smile. "It was your journey."

"But I went there. Really I did. What does it mean?"

"It means a lot," said Dennis. "You have made your journey and learned the lessons you had to learn. What did you learn?"

"I don't know," he responded. "I learned not to be afraid, I guess."

They ate without speaking. Afterwards Lawrence helped Dennis clean up and then folded his blanket. Saying good-by, he left the cabin and slowly walked down into the arroyo toward town, lost in thought.

"It was so real," he said out loud. "But it must have been a dream after all."

Suddenly, he felt a stinging in his side. He quickly reached under his belt and pulled out a piece of wood, no more than a quarter inch long, pointy at one end and with a crude handle at the other end. He stared at it for the longest time. Then he slowly smiled, put it in his pocket, and ran for home.

CPSIA information can be obtained at www.ICGtesting.com
Printed in the USA
BVOW03s1356270414

351807BV00001B/154/P